"I'm willing to take on the job," Judi said

His cool look assessed her. "I could use you, provided you can take the heat and the humidity and still do a good job."

Use her. Like a piece of his photographic equipment. Judi threw him a look of pure dislike. "It wouldn't work out."

She had started to turn away when Nick Compton drawled, "Do you always back out when the going gets rough?"

His taunt stopped Judi in her tracks. "I know better than to try to fill a leaking bucket."

Dave had said they were both fire signs, she and Nick, whatever that meant. One thing was sure, on each occasion they had clashed it was she, Judi, who had been burned.

The next time, she vowed, she would make sure it was Nick who was scorched instead....

Angela Carson has been writing Harlequin Romances for the last few years, and the quality of her writing and her interesting characters have attracted many readers. She lives in the countryside near Birmingham, England, where as well as writing she is able to indulge her love of gardening.

Books by Angela Carson

ANOTHER MAN'S RING

Angela Carson

Harlequin Books

TORONTO • NEW YORK • LONDON
AMSTERDAM • PARIS • SYDNEY • HAMBURG
STOCKHOLM • ATHENS • TOKYO • MILAN

Original hardcover edition published in 1989
by Mills & Boon Limited

ISBN 0-373-03067-3

Harlequin Romance first edition August 1990

CHAPTER ONE

'I'M at my wits' end, Louise. I've got to stop it somehow, and I don't know how.'

'Stop what?'

'Me, getting married to Robert.'

'But you've only just got engaged.'

'I know. The holiday we had to celebrate our engagement woke me up to some hard facts, and I don't like any single one of them.'

Judi shivered, her brown eyes dark with the memory of that disastrous trip to India, which had changed her mind, and left her in the dilemma which now confronted her.

Her friend Louise said cautiously, 'Marriages don't always last too long, nowadays.'

'If ever I get married, mine's going to last a lifetime,' Judi vowed fiercely. 'But not to Robert.'

'Have you told him how you feel?'

'Not yet. I've got to think of a way out, first. He's mad keen on the engagement. But now I know why, I'm not.'

'Surely he got engaged because he loves you?' Louise took in Judi's scornful snort, and placated, 'Engagements aren't a final commitment, anyway. There're meant to be more of a trial period. Let it run on for a while, until all the excitement has died away, and then, if you still feel the same way, give Robert his ring back, and tell him it won't work.'

'It isn't as easy as that,' said Judi gloomily. 'Both sets of parents have erupted in an absolute rash of wedding fever, and Robert's egging them on. They're planning a wedding before Christmas.'

'I didn't think you wanted it so soon.'

'I don't want it at all, now. But what I want, or don't want, doesn't seem to count.'

'Is there—er—any special reason for their haste?' Louise questioned delicately, and Judi flashed her friend an indignant look.

'A baby on the way, do you mean? No, I wouldn't. Not before I was married.'

'Then I don't see why...'

'It's purely a matter of business, not love,' she said bitterly. 'You know Robert's people own that big hardware chain? Well, there's been talk of a closer liaison between their firm and my father's supermarkets for some time. Apparently competition from abroad is getting tougher, and to fight off the opposition it will pay them to merge. Me getting married to Robert is a neat way of making sure the contract won't fall through.'

'Surely your family can't be so cold-blooded? You seemed to be so happy together before you got engaged.'

'I was. It was the classic example of living in a fool's paradise. And what a fool I have been. But I had no reason, then, to suspect that Robert might have an ulterior motive for his attentions. And he was attentive. He seemed as if he could not spend enough time with me. His father gave him endless time off from work, just so that we could be together. It was a sprat to catch a mackerel. Both our parents gave us all the encouragement they could, and I was naïve enough to believe that they were only interested in my happiness. Now, I know better.'

'Are you sure you're not just over-reacting? Now the excitement of getting engaged is over, things are bound to fall a bit flat.'

'Over-reacting?' Judi's laugh held no humour. 'On the contrary, I'm only just beginning to wake up. Funnily enough, it was the newspaper publicity which surrounded our engagement that struck the first sour note. Do you remember the headlines?'

Louise nodded thoughtfully. She remembered them vividly, and had wondered about them herself.

'Link Between Two High Street Giants' they had read, and the articles below the headlines had been more about the merging of the two firms than about the happy couple themselves.

This half of the couple looked distinctly unhappy as she went on, 'The toasts at our engagement party were the same. The first one was to the proposed merger, and then they toasted Robert and me as a sort of afterthought.'

'They might have felt a bit euphoric about having both things happen at once.'

'That's what I tried to tell myself. But while Robert and I were on holiday in India, supposed to be celebrating our engagement, he spent most of the time in business discussions with the various firms his company has got links with out there, while I kicked my heels in outer offices, waiting for him to emerge. All he could talk about was the bright future for the two companies. He should have been talking about my future—our future...' Judi's voice choked to a halt, but after a couple of hard swallows she forced it on. 'It was as if, now he had got what he wanted,

Robert switched off from me. Every day he had a telephone call from his office to tell him how the merger negotiations were progressing, and when they were all ready and due to be signed, he cut short our holiday so that he could be there to add his signature to the contract. I feel like the parchment it's been written on. And since we've been back, Robert has shown up in his true colours. Everything has to give way to business. There's no time for this or that, because of meetings. No time for me . . .'

'Stand up for yourself,' Louise told her briskly. 'Put a brake on the wedding arrangements until you've had time to calm down and think things over. A wedding before Christmas is rushing things a bit. Even your parents must realise that.'

'Oh, that's nothing. The two fathers are going even faster. They've already decided that our first child must be a boy, to take over the joint firms eventually. And the rush is for financial reasons. The shares of the two companies have risen because of the news of our engagement, and they want to "consolidate a favourable climate" before the first annual general meeting of the merged firm. I think that's the correct business phraseology. It's even beginning to infect me, now.'

A note of hysteria invaded Judi's voice as she went on, 'I feel trapped, Louise. The pressure is awful, and it's getting worse every day.'

'Talk to your parents.'

'You know that's not possible. They're worse, if anything, than Robert and his family. But I didn't think they would ever go so far as to use me in this way.'

Louise wished she had not made the useless suggestion, and she remained silent as Judi continued, 'I've tried to put the brake on, but Mother refuses to listen. Nothing must stand in the way of the merger. I'm beginning to feel like a pawn in some dreadful game of human chess.'

'You can't allow it to go on while you feel like this,' said Louise firmly. 'You're a human being, not a business asset. You mustn't allow yourself to be used as mortar to bind together Bartlett Holdings, and what-d'you-call-it plc, no matter how much the families might want the merger.'

'You've put the whole thing in a nutshell. I feel like a share being bought and sold on the Stock Exchange, but everything's happening so fast, it's like trying to swim against a tidal wave.'

'Have a drink of this to keep you afloat, while we think of some way out.'

Louise handed a cup of strong coffee over the desk, and her kindly eyes hardened as the dark liquid almost slopped over the rim under the tremble of Judi's small hands. The stress it betrayed accelerated Louise's nimble mind to lightning speed, and she offered the solution, 'If you can't swim against the tide, then duck under the surface, out of sight, for a while. That should steady them down, and give you time to think things out for yourself. They can't plan a wedding without a bride.'

'If only I could,' said Judi wistfully. 'But it's finding some place to duck into.'

'You could come with hubby and me on our walking-tour.'

'Long-distance trekking isn't really my forte. Besides, aren't you going to visit one of your husband's relatives in remotest somewhere-or-other, half-way through your holiday?'

'Shropshire.'

Louise nodded, and Judi went on forcefully, 'I've had it up to here with my own family for the moment. I just don't feel I can take any more relatives, whoever they belong to.'

She sketched an apologetic level near to her small chin, to take the sting from her words. She felt angry and bitter at the way in which she had been used, and it showed as she finished wearily, 'A desert island would be magic for me right now.'

'Then I'll wave the wand for you.' Louise waved her hand airily. 'I can't offer you a desert island, but a week from now you will be transported to Thailand,' she announced grandly.

'Thailand? You must be joking.'

'I'm deadly serious. Drink your coffee, instead of staring at it as if it were a pool you wish you could jump into, and listen.' Louise took a drink from her own mug, and leaning her elbows on the desk she began, 'The language school shall be your magic carpet.'

She referred flippantly to the small but exclusive business which she ran for the benefit of the children of diplomats and businessmen temporarily located in England, which had gained such a well-deserved reputation that she now had a permanent waiting-list of pupils.

Faced with expansion, she had called upon Judi to help her, remembering that her schoolfriend had taken a secretarial course for no better reason than that using a typewriter was less laborious than writing up her class notes by hand.

Under their joint efforts, the small enterprise had flourished, and, as Louise saw it, could now well offer her friend the escape route she sought.

She went on swiftly, 'You know the two children of the Thai businessman? The ones in the second grade?' Judi nodded, and Louise went on, 'Things have been happening while you were in India. Their father has been called home to take up a promotion. His wife's baby is due any moment now, so he sent her off early, so that the child can be born in its own country, and he was going to take the other two children with him a week from now.'

'Isn't he going, after all?'

'Yes, but later. There's been a minor snag to his clearing up arrangements over here. But the children are so excited about being at home when the new baby arrives, he didn't want to disappoint them and cancel their flight, so he's asked me to provide an escort to take them home, and he will follow on his own when he's straightened out matters at this end. How do you feel about being the escort?' she asked with a twinkle.

'Do you really mean it, Louise? It's just what I need. Although it wouldn't keep me away for long,' she realised, her quick uprush of relief fading.

'You needn't come back right away. Hand over the two children, and then stay on and give yourself a holiday. You look as if you need one. And you've already had all the necessary jabs for your trip to India with Robert.'

That holiday had been so brief that the tan had already faded. Not so the doubts which had started then, and still tormented her. Judi said gloomily, 'Robert might want to come as well. There might be some business opportunities for him over there.'

'Surely he will be at that trade fair, with your parents and his?'

Judi's face cleared. 'Of course. I'd forgotten.'

'Well, then, leave a note saying I've asked you to escort two pupils back home in an emergency. That's stretching the truth a bit, but under the circumstances I think it's justified. Say you'll come back some time, and simply forget to say when, or where from.'

'Robert will come straight here to find out where I've gone to.'

'The school will be closed for the holiday, and I can disappear on our walking-trip a few days early, so he'll have no luck. How's that for a solution to your problem?' She grinned, and Judi's eyes sparked in response.

'What about travel documents and things?' She still did not dare to allow herself to hope.

'Thai businessmen can pull strings, as well as tycoons, on this side of the water,' Louise responded drily. 'Leave it to him.'

The pulled strings must have been effective, because a week later Judi boarded a Thai Airways flight with two children in tow, and a guilty urge to look over her shoulder to make sure that neither her parents nor her fiancé were in pursuit.

Her hastily scribbled note, dictated by Louise, lay in her father's study awaiting his return after their weekend away, but now that her escape was accomplished, anticlimax set in, and Judi's mind became a confusion of conflicting thoughts as the long hours of the flight wore on.

Nervously she twisted the large solitaire diamond ring round and round on her engagement finger. She wished now that she had left it behind at home, but if she had, and her mother had discovered it in her dressing-table drawer, it would have fuelled an immediate uproar, so on reflection she had kept the ring on her finger, and decided to deposit it in the hotel safe immediately she arrived.

Her charges slept peacefully, but her own overcharged emotions denied her rest. She knew exactly what she was escaping from. But what was she escaping to?

Until her engagement, she had been content with helping Louise to make a success of the language school, and enjoying her social life with Robert and their circle of friends, with the future stretching securely before her, but not much occupying her mind.

Now, it intruded, and refused to go away. Inevitably she would have to return to England. And then what? Robert apart, what did she, Judi, really want from life?

Did she want to remain at the language school indefinitely, working away the years as its administrator, however interesting the job might be? The prospect stretching before her seemed as bleak as a future spent with Robert.

The question buzzed in her mind for the rest of the flight, with the irritating persistence of a mosquito. What shape did she want her life to take from now on? Perhaps her stay in Thailand might provide her with the answer.

The children received a rapturous welcome when they reached their journey's end the next morning. Their uncle rescued the small party from the clamour of taxi-drivers at Bangkok airport, where the heat hit them like a solid wall, making Judi thankful to dive into the comparative shelter of the large air-conditioned limousine awaiting them.

A fraught hour later, and after the most horrendous traffic jams she had ever seen, Judi felt glad to escape still intact from the car.

Bangkok drivers performed at a suicidal level that made her long to shut her eyes. Each driver cheerfully leaned on his horn without attempting to slacken speed, relying on the ear-splitting din it created to gain him the right of way. Since all the others did the same, it created a cacophony of noise that set Judi's jet-lagged nerves jangling.

The children's uncle smiled imperturbably through it all, and Judi envied him the ability, and had to take her courage in both hands later to accept his offer of a lift to her hotel, where the family had booked her in for a couple of nights at their expense.

They were due to travel up country to their own home the next morning, leaving Judi to her own devices; and she went from her second experience of the maelstrom of Bangkok traffic into the calm of the hotel lobby, vowing to make the most of her time in this hitherto unvisited country.

The hotel which had been chosen for her was a reflection of the Thai family's wealth, and Judi planned privately to enjoy the luxury while it lasted, and then to remove herself to a less expensive abode and to stay on for as long as her funds lasted.

Her air tickets were open-ended, with no fixed date for her return, and she had taken out a tourist visa for the longest time allowed, with no clear idea of how far her money would stretch, but only knowing that she did not intend to return to England until she was absolutely obliged to.

With lifting spirits she completed the formalities at the hotel reception desk, and dictated a telex to Louise at the school to reassure her that her two small pupils were now safely in the care of their mother.

That done, she handed over her engagement ring, saw it deposited in the hotel safe, and felt as if a tremendous weight had been lifted from her mind as well as her finger as she accepted the receipt for her jewellery, and turned to sign the register with a heady feeling of freedom.

She retracted the end of her ball-point pen, and slid it back into her handbag as a deep male voice enquired of the receptionist in English, 'Can you possibly provide us with a secretary? It's short notice, I know, but we've just heard that the girl who was to join our team has been obliged to cry off at the last minute, and we need help right away.'

Forced to wait for the receptionist to hand over her room-key, Judi had no option but to stand by and listen as the girl asked politely, 'What kind of secretarial work is entailed, sir?'

'My boss needs someone who is willing to travel along with him, and take dictation on the hoof. He has to give a potted description of every photograph he takes, and they all have to be typed and collated. There are too many for him to be able to waste time doing the nitty-gritty himself.'

'I'll try, Mr Metcalf, but it might be difficult. All our senior secretarial staff are already on loan to that big international conference that is being held in the city. One of the other hotels might have someone they can send, but it's doubtful. They've been swamped with requests by the delegates for secretarial services, and all the best girls have already been booked.'

The receptionist took the sting from her words with the now familiar wide smile, and Judi wondered if all the Thai women were as beautiful and serene as the ones she had encountered so far. She felt positively clumsy beside their exquisite grace.

The man called Metcalf frowned. 'We must get a fully experienced girl who's first-class at her job. She'll need to be able to take down shorthand at a fast talking-speed, and it's essential that she speaks perfect English, because that's what all the brochure blurbs are to be written in. Any translations that are needed will be done back at base.'

Listening to the stranger's plaint, a mad, crazy notion gripped Judi, and before common sense could assert itself she swung round impulsively to face the speaker, and declared, 'I can take down shorthand at nearly two hundred words a minute, and I speak perfect English. And I'm available, and willing, now.'

'Lady, in this country that sort of statement could get you into instant trouble.'

Shrewd eyes in a hard-bitten face turned to survey Judi. Briefly they surveyed her smooth bob, the nut-brown hair glinting with pure gold, then they lingered on the petite figure that Judi knew to her chagrin made her look several years younger than she was.

The man obviously got that impression, because he emphasised, 'I need an *experienced* secretary.'

Judi's face flamed. The meaning of his first remark had just sunk in, and it made the disbelief of his second seem to pale by comparison.

'I didn't mean ... I ...' She choked to a mortified halt, and instantly he took up her thoughts.

'No offence meant. But you need to be careful. You don't look old enough ...'

'I'm twenty-three,' Judi clipped, already regretting her impulsiveness. She had no idea who this man was, what his team were, or where they came from, let alone what they were doing in Thailand. The man spoke, and brought her confused thoughts to a halt.

'So, you *are* twenty-three.' Ignoring Judi's gasp of indignation, he picked up her passport, opened it and inspected its pages. 'You're down here as an administrator. Administrating what?'

'A language school.'

'Languages, eh? Do you speak Thai?'

'No. I administrate. I don't teach.'

'Pity. It would have been an advantage. But it isn't essential.' He smiled, suddenly, and without quite knowing why Judi found herself smiling back. 'I'm David Metcalf,' he said, and held out his hand. 'Call me Dave. And you're...mmm, Judi Bartlett. How come you're in Thailand, Judi? Are you on holiday?'

'No, I came over to escort two of our pupils back home. Now I've delivered them to their family I'm free to stay on for a while, and I couldn't help overhearing your difficulty.'

'So you're on your own here?'

'Yes.'

It was not the most sensible admission to make in a strange country, even to an obvious compatriot, but it was something he could soon check for himself, so there was no point in pretending otherwise. Judi saw no reason why she should also explain her reluctance to return home. Fortune seemed to be smiling on her, and she silently thanked the impulse that had made her apply for an extended visa, and eyed Dave hopefully. If she could land this job, however temporary, it would do her more of a good turn than it would his boss.

'It's Nick's difficulty more than mine,' Dave said. 'It will be up to him to have the final say when he's met you, but I should say the two of you would get on all right together.' Briefly, his eyes flicked downwards again on to her passport. 'I see you're a Sagittarian.'

'A what?'

'A Sagittarian.' The keen eyes twinkled. 'A sign of the zodiac. Your birthday's in December.'

'Oh, that. What's that got to do with anything?'

'A lot, in Thailand. They're strong on astrology over here. Didn't you know?'

She could not tell from his expression whether he was serious or not. 'This is the first time I've been in Thailand,' she hedged, and he nodded.

'It's easy to see you haven't spent a lot of time in a hot climate.' His look appreciated her fine skin, and deepened the rose tint in her cheeks, and he smiled again and said, 'You'd better come and meet Nick, and see what he says. For your information, he's a Leo.'

'What's that supposed to mean?'

'It means you two will click—get along together,' he answered confidently, and added, 'You're both fire signs, too,' as if the getting along together might not be without some interesting sparks.

Judi's look dismissed his fantasising, and he shrugged. 'Suit yourself. But it works, whether you believe it or not.' He took her key from the receptionist, glanced at the tab before handing it to Judi, and added, 'Your room is along the same corridor as

ours. I'll walk you up, and explain on the way what
we're all about.'

His explanation was reassuring, and went a long
way to quell Judi's misgivings about her wisdom in
applying for the job. Dave told her, 'There are four
of us on the team altogether. At least, there would
have been four, if the secretary had turned up. We've
been commissioned by an upmarket travel firm to
produce a set of brochures on tours in Thailand.'

He mentioned the name of an extremely upmarket
travel firm that raised Judi's eyebrows. She knew the
holidays they offered were a far cry from the run-of-
the-mill package tours. They were the modern equiv-
alent of the Grand Tour, aimed at the very wealthy,
with no expense spared, with glossy brochures that
were works of art in themselves. Before she could
comment, Dave went on, 'Pet and I are both employed on their regular staff. I sort out the travel arrangements for the tours, and Pet looks after the
accommodation and food and so on. Nick's a
freelance. He's leading the team because of his in-
timate knowledge of the country. He's doing all the
brochure photography, and the historical blurbs that
go with the pictures, which is why he needs a secretary.'

'Do you mean, to research the facts about whatever
he photographs?'

'No, just to take them down in shorthand, while
he's busy taking the picture. That way, the two can
be linked up easily at the other end, with no possibility of a mistake. He's a perfectionist, is Nick, as
well as being an authority on the Far East. Professor
Nicholas Compton, to give him his full title, with a
string of letters after his name, and the travel firm
were jolly lucky to get him. He's a freelance writer,

photographer, lecturer . . . you name it. He can pick
and choose the jobs he does. The firm only got him
to do this one because he happens to love Thailand,
and didn't trust any old photographer to do justice
to it.'

Judi digested the information in silence. The only
professor of her acquaintance was old and bearded,
which added to the reassurance. Although this particular one sounded arrogant.

Leo the lion, and thinks he's the cat's whiskers, and
no one but he can take good photographs, she thought
scornfully. Oh, well, it would make a change from
ordering textbooks for the school, and if she landed
the job it would conserve her own funds, and keep
her out of reach of Robert and her family for longer
than she would have been able to afford otherwise.

She made a mental note to look up Robert's star
sign when she returned home. Dave did not look as
if anyone could pull the wool over his eyes, and he
seemed to believe in astrology, so perhaps there was
something in it, after all. Maybe she and Robert were
incompatible for that reason. And maybe, just maybe,
he and their mutual families might take that as a good
reason for her not to get married to him.

Now it was she who was fantasising. Judi shrugged
her thoughts into submission as her companion paused
before a room door and asked, 'Do you want to go
to your room first, or will you come in and meet Nick
right away?'

'I'll come in and meet him,' Judi decided. Best to
get the interview over, so that she would know her
fate before she settled in.

Dave pushed open the door, and called out, 'Nick,
your luck's in. I've found a secretary for you. She

writes shorthand in the fast lane, and what's more, she's available right away.' He did not add 'willing', but his eyes swivelled to tease Judi, kindly, and this time she did not mind. 'Professor Nick Compton,' he introduced, and waved his hand towards the so far unseen occupant of the room, while removing his own bulk from in front of Judi to allow her a view.

She blinked. The professor's luck might be in, but her own definitely was not, she decided, aghast. This particular academic was neither old, nor bearded. He was young and virile, thirty-two or three at the most, and clean-shaven, and Judi stared at him in undisguised dismay.

Nick Compton was no stranger to her. They had met once, several months ago, and that disastrously, and their clash had left a dent in her self-esteem that still smarted.

Did he remember their meeting on that snowy morning in late spring? For her part, it was impossible to forget the tawny head with its thick thatch of wavy hair above a high forehead, and the deep-set, burning golden eyes, like banked fires, in the lean face, that fixed her feet to the spot, and made her wish she could dive back behind the shelter of Dave's bulky form.

Leo was a perfect description of the professor, she thought, shaken. The last time they met, he had roared at her with unmistakable fury. She had bitten back, and their brief encounter had left a wound that still stung.

Nick Compton gave Judi a long, assessing look that seemed to go on forever before he made it clear that he, too, remembered. 'We're already acquainted,' he told his colleague, and threw at Judi, 'I hope your office skills are better than your driving.'

He did not pull his punches now, any more than he had then. Judi's hope of getting the job evaporated, but spiritedly she fought back.

'It wasn't my fault. Anyone is likely to skid on hard-packed ice.'

She was aware of Dave's puzzled look, and thought, so much for his faith in the signs of the zodiac.

'*I* didn't skid.'

The arrogant statement aroused Judi's wrath. She glared at this creature who, a few seconds ago, she had unwisely hoped would offer her a job. 'Your car had got more weight than mine. It would hold the road better.'

'Your Mini packed quite a clout.'

'It didn't do any damage to your car. And I said I was sorry.'

What else could she say, when she had backed hard into the pristine bumper of this man's brand-new Jaguar V12 convertible, in the tight space of a mid-town parking slot?

Even in the sub-zero temperature at the time, she'd noticed that the car had had its hood down, and the low-slung, crimson metallic body reflected the lithe speed of its outraged owner, as he catapulted from the driving-seat and proceeded to spell out to Judi, in no uncertain terms, his opinion of her driving abilities.

'If you had, you would have picked up the bill.'

Judi gave a gasp. The incident was months ago. Did the man never forget? They said elephants never forgot. Perhaps it applied to lions, as well. She felt an irreverent urge to giggle, and then met Nick

Compton's look; the urge died a hurried death, but her anger against him remained.

That single, unfortunate motoring contretemps, on an atrocious surface, did not give him the right to transfer his opinion of her driving to her as a person. He knew nothing whatsoever about Judi herself.

Nothing? Those burning, amber eyes saw in and through her, and read everything about her. With an effort Judi dragged her gaze away from them and turned to Dave.

'I'll go along to my own room now. You were wrong. It wouldn't work out.'

She had started to turn away when Nick Compton drawled, 'Do you always back out when the going gets rough?'

His taunt stopped Judi in her tracks. 'I know better than to try to fill a leaking bucket.'

He shrugged. 'Suit yourself. A secretary who's going to wilt the moment she goes outside an air-conditioned hotel is no good to me.'

'I don't wilt in the heat. I've been in a hot climate before. In fact, I'm only just back from India.'

'So?'

His cool look assessed her lack of suntan, and Judi flared, 'So I'm willing to take on the job, if you want me to.'

'I could use you, provided you can take the heat and the humidity, and still do a good job of work.'

Use her. Like a piece of his photographic equipment. Judi threw him a look of pure dislike. She did not need Dave's description of Nick to tell her that he would be infinitely demanding.

At least he was honest, she gave him that. He did not try to cover up his motives, as Robert had done.

Her fiancé had used her shamelessly, as had her own family. She still felt stunned at their treatment, but now the pain was turning to anger against them, and a deep relief that she had not allowed Robert to make final use of her, as he had wanted to while they were in India, no doubt as a seal to cement the bargain between the two firms. Her lips twisted, remembering her adamant, '*No*, Robert.'

'But we're engaged.'

'We're not married yet. I'm just not that type.'

If she had given in to his demands, the result might have made it impossible for her to break free, whereas now by comparison it would be merely difficult and unpleasant and... She thrust future confrontations from her, and faced this one with a determined, 'I won't wilt. And as for my work, you'll just have to take me on trust, Professor Compton, the same as I'll have to take you.' She said it sweetly, and had the satisfaction of seeing the gold eyes fire.

The learned professor was obviously not used to being spoken to in such a disrespectful manner, and the responsive flare gave Judi great satisfaction.

Eyeing him covertly, she wondered just how far she would be able to trust Nick Compton. With his tall, athletic frame and unusual colouring he was a handsome animal, and no doubt very well aware of the fact, and of his impact upon members of the opposite sex.

In spite of her dislike of him, Judi felt the impact herself, loud and clear, and was thankful that she was immune. For the moment, anyway, she'd had more than enough of men, however good-looking.

Nick cut across her thoughts. 'It's a deal, then. And call me Nick. I'll see you at dinner, and tell you anything else you need to know then.'

He dismissed her in typically royal fashion, as befitted a king of the beasts. Judi's ruffled sensibilities eradicated 'king', and she fulminated, 'Beast!' as she dressed for dinner later.

She had no doubts about her ability to cope with whatever work her new boss might throw in her direction, and the opportunity to join in a virtual lecture tour of this exotic country was too good to be missed.

She would remain as Nick's secretary for just long enough to do that, she decided. It would give her time to decide on her future after she returned home, which in turn would make it easier for her to end her engagement and face the storm which she knew ruefully must be weathered sooner or later. She would use Nick as he intended to use her, and gain added satisfaction from making him eat his poor opinion of her.

She had still to meet the other member of the team. She wondered idly what Pet would be like. Was it a term of endearment, or a shortened form of her real name? Judi wondered. Both men used it. Nick said, when he took his seat at the table directly opposite to Judi, 'Pet's gone to try out the food at the Gulf this evening. You'll meet her tomorrow.'

His look appraised Judi's cool, cream-coloured cotton dress, with the gaily patterned jacket that was still a welcome addition to combat the evening chill at this late end of the rainy season. She had bought it for India, and knew that she looked good in it, and it gave her the confidence to endure his stare until he transferred it to the menu, and told her, 'Order whatever you like.'

'I'll have the same as you.'

Left to her own devices, Judi would have explored the Thai dishes only after consultation with the waiter, because, never having visited the country before, she was unsure of the contents.

Robert always ate unadventurously English food, even when they were in India, and her only incursions so far into the realms of Eastern food were confined to occasional forays with Louise into ethnic restaurants near to the language school, and in the company of her new boss she did not relish making a fool of herself by ordering something that might turn out to be too way out for her to cope with.

Dave chuckled, and said, 'Watch it. Nick likes Thai food just as it comes, hot and spicy.'

Nick said, 'Let her try it, if she wants to,' and taunted Judi, when she hesitated with her spoon poised above an unidentifiable steaming plateful a few minutes later, 'It's food for the daring.'

Had he chosen it deliberately to test her?

Judi raised her eyes to his across the table, and stared at him from under her long, silky lashes that borrowed the gold at their tips from the rich glints in her hair.

Anyone looking out from under the shelter of such lashes should view what they saw through a golden halo, but she saw no such angelic ring around her dinner companion. A halo would not sit comfortably on that narrow, intelligent head with its flat ears slightly pointed at the tips, like the buds of tiny horns, giving him a satanic appearance that accorded with her view of him so far.

The mingled spicy aromas from her plate rose to tantalise her nostrils, tempting her to adventure. Nick's stare from across the table held her gaze, challenging her, and suddenly Judi knew that his challenge was not only for her to eat the food he had chosen.

The glow, deep in those golden orbs, held the prospect of other, more dangerous fare, fraught with peril for the one who was tempted to eat.

Judi felt tempted, but did she dare?

The question loaded the air between them. Nick sat absolutely still, not touching his own meal, silently waiting for her to decide how she would answer.

Food for the daring...

Instinct cautioned Judi that if she tasted, and scorched her mouth in the process, there was no guarantee that Nick would offer her any balm for the pain.

She could not help wondering what form such balm would take, if he did. As if in answer, her eyes were drawn to the perfectly cut line of his lips, the corners turned upwards now in a slight satirical smile at her expense.

Would they be the ones to press the pain away from her mouth?

She knew with an unshakable conviction that they would try. And, when they did, one taste might not be enough, and the penalty might far outweigh the pleasure.

Only she could choose.

Nick waited without moving, and as if in a dream Judi felt her hand begin to lower her spoon to her plate. Still held by his stare, she slowly dipped it, raised the contents to her mouth, and tasted.

The curry set her tongue on fire. Sheets of flame blasted her throat and took the roof off her mouth, and Judi felt convinced that her teeth must be melting in the searing heat. She gagged and choked, and her eyes began to stream, and she reached blindly for the water jug to douse the furnace raging inside her.

In a panic of agony she heard Nick's chuckle, and hated him with a fierce loathing that shocked her. If this was his way of getting back at her for pranging his brand new car, he had succeeded beyond his wildest expectations, and it was her own stupid fault for falling for his ploy.

Judi gulped water, mopped her streaming eyes clear, glared at him across the table, and met laughter and something else, which she could not define, stirring in the golden stare; it sent the fire from her throat to scorch the blood in her veins, causing her pulses to leap in a way in which no other man, certainly not Robert, had been able to make them behave before.

Judi scorned their gymnastics now. The pain subsided slightly, restoring some of her poise, and Nick could not know how her pulses still raced. She did not know whether to be glad or sorry that she had tasted. She felt exhilarated, and strangely afraid.

And, disconcertingly, she knew an overpowering urge to taste again, regardless of the consequences, if only to prove herself to this impossible creature, who humiliatingly had won the first two rounds of their encounter so far.

What was it Dave had said of them? That they were both fire signs, whatever that meant. One thing was sure, on each occasion they had clashed it was she, Judi, who had been the one burned.

The next time, she vowed, she would make sure it was Nick who was scorched instead.

CHAPTER TWO

DAVE introduced Pet at breakfast the next morning.

'Petra Welsh. Judi Bartlett, Nick's new secretary,' he announced, and an older woman, already seated at the table, raised pale blue eyes as Judi sat down beside Dave.

Pet made no attempt to shake hands, and offered only a brief nod, and said, 'I thought you had to cry off coming at the last minute.'

As a welcome it did not rate very high, and Judi answered briefly, 'Not me.'

Dave cut in, 'The secretary we originally engaged couldn't come, and Judi stepped into the breach. She was in the hotel lobby while I was trying to get a re-placement, and offered to help out.'

'I told Nick it wouldn't be necessary for him to get a girl on this trip. I offered to do his odds and ends of typing for him.'

'Be thankful I didn't take you up on your offer,' Nick said, and slid into the vacant seat beside Pet. 'You've got your work cut out as it is, coping with your own brief. I want more than just odds and ends of typing.'

He said 'want' and not 'need', and his direct look at Judi as he said it told her that he had chosen his words deliberately. She wondered uneasily what the difference entailed in his estimation. She could feel his eyes rake her face, bringing the ready colour to stain her cheeks, and hurriedly she lowered her eyes, using her lashes as shields against his enigmatic stare.

Her brief would not be all plain sailing with this man, but she was engaged as his secretary, and his wants and needs must be kept strictly within those limits, she determined. She welcomed the timely arrival of the waiter which brought an end to the subject, and turned the conversation on to food instead as the man took their breakfast orders.

Nick stirred his coffee and asked Pet, 'How did you find the Gulf last night?'

'The facilities were first-class,' Pet replied, 'and the food was out of this world. I'm definitely going to add it on to my list of "musts".'

Pet obviously enjoyed that part of her work, Judi decided cattily. The older woman's thin cotton garments strained at all the wrong places. Judi judged her age to be nearing forty, in spite of her carefully touched-up blonde hair, a disastrous time of life to over-indulge in the calories, and it showed.

Perhaps Judi's lissom figure had something to do with Pet's lack of welcome. Or, more likely, since she appeared to be so eager to help with Nick's work on top of her own, she fancied the photographer.

Dave was more her age, if she wanted a man, Judi thought. And he was nice, too, which was a bonus. Of the two men, she herself infinitely preferred Dave, though not in that way. The square-set figure, toughened by all the discomforts of global travel known to human endurance, would not see forty again, and Judi felt glad he was a part of the team. She sensed that she was going to need an antidote to the abrasive company of the other two.

Nick presented unplumbed depths. Judi surveyed him surreptitiously. She needed no instinct to warn her that she would rapidly find herself in difficulties if she was tempted to try to swim those depths, and Pet's cold unwelcome was surely aimed not at Judi herself so much as at any younger, good-looking woman who might pose a threat in the older woman's eyes.

She need not worry, Judi thought hardily. She had enough man problems of her own, without taking on board any more. She wondered, as she nibbled her single slice of toast, how Pet could possibly cope with a full cooked breakfast when she knew that she would be going out into the heat of the streets almost immediately afterwards.

Nick had not said anything yet about his plans for the day, and whether or not they would include herself. As if he read her thoughts, he remedied the omission with, 'I want to get one or two of the more conventional shots of Bangkok today. What are your plans, Pet?'

'I'll come with you.'

'There's no point in trailing along in this heat if you don't have to. Judi will do all that's necessary for me. You've still got a couple of hotels to check out, and if you've got any time to spare, you might as well take the chance of a rest before we move up country.'

A concession to Pet's advancing years? Judi wondered with an inward grin, which must have shown in her expression because Pet glared at her from across the table as Nick qualified, 'Dave might be glad of your help, though. He's checking out the final travel arrangements for the number one tour, and he'll need someone to find out for him what sort of facilities are laid on for females during the journey.'

Females. Judi gritted her teeth. Nick Compton was not only a beast, he was a chauvinist too. The allusion did not seem to register with Pet, however, because she persisted, 'It won't take me long to run through the other hotels. I could meet up with you later.'

She should know better, Judi thought, watching with interest the beginnings of a frown on Nick's high forehead. It did not reach his voice, however, which remained amiable but quite adamant as he answered, 'We'll meet up this evening. Dave was telling me you'd booked us into that big restaurant with the floor-show.'

'Yes, it's good. I'd like you to see it.'

Pet's 'you' excluded Judi and Dave, and her vitriolic look followed Judi to the door when Nick rose and said, 'If you've finished your breakfast, Judi, we might as well get going while it's still comparatively cool. I hope you've got some comfortable footwear.'

'I'm suitably equipped. I told you, I'm not a stranger to a hot climate.'

'But you've still got a lot to learn,' he taunted, and made Judi want to hit him.

The episode of the curry still rankled. Her mouth and throat had returned to normal this morning, but her nerves still jangled at the memory of Nick signalling to an amused waiter to remove the fiery plateful and replace it with another very much milder version of the same dish.

'I'll finish this one,' she had protested, but Nick had overruled her.

'I can't afford to have a member of the team go down with a stomach upset. From now on, stick to what you can handle.'

Had he intended the warning to apply to himself as well as to the food?

Judi's eyes flew to his face, but it remained expressionless, giving nothing away as he added, 'I'll meet you in reception in ten minutes.'

He was there before her, and Judi appraised him as she descended the stairs exactly ten minutes later, unwilling to be seen meekly waiting for him to appear, but equally unwilling to be even a second over the time and give him the opportunity to criticise her.

His lack of equipment surprised her. Her own photographic efforts were of the click and hope-for-the-best variety, but with visions of tourists hung about with photographic equipment like mobile Christmas trees she was surprised at the neat proportions of the holdall slung over Nick's broad shoulder.

The only clue to his professionalism was the expensive-looking camera which she had noticed on the table in his room the day before, and which now rested at the end of its neck-strap against his taut, muscled midriff, ready for instant use.

His leonine head rose as she appeared round the bend of the wide, curved stairway, and he watched her coolly as she descended.

Confusedly Judi wished that Dave, or even Pet, would appear and speak to him. Anything to distract his attention, and make him look away from her, would be welcome. His silent regard caused her feet to become clumsy. She stumbled and, fearful of tripping and landing in an undignified heap at his feet, she reached out a hand to the banister for support, hating the quick flash of amusement that lit his face, telling her that he knew he was the cause.

With an effort she pulled herself together, and achieved the last stair, resisting the urge to hurry, and said briskly, 'I'm ready when you are.'

For answer he held out a small piece of pasteboard towards her, and said, 'Put this somewhere safely in your bag before we go out, in case we accidentally get separated during the day.'

Judi took it from him. It was one of the cards from the rack on the reception desk, and bore the name, address and telephone number of the hotel.

'I don't need this. I can remember where I'm staying.'

'Put it in your bag just the same, and don't lose it,' he commanded. 'This isn't Spain. English isn't widely spoken in Thailand. Even with the taxi drivers, you might have difficulty in making yourself understood, but these cards are printed in English and Thai, and they'll get you out of trouble if you happen to get lost. So do as you are told, and don't argue. I haven't got the time or the inclination to go looking for a missing secretary.'

Judi had to remind herself firmly that this was what she now was, his secretary, and she must school herself not to bristle each time he requested her to do something. It was just that Nick's requests came in the unmistakable form of orders, which rasped her independent spirit.

Under his watchful stare she reluctantly opened her shoulder-bag and zipped the card into a side pocket, and he nodded his satisfaction. 'That should be safe enough in there, so long as you don't lose your bag.'

Her head shot up, but he stopped her indignant rejoiner with the observation, 'I see you've brought along your own camera.'

She could not deny it, since it lay in the open top of her bag; it was a popular model from one of her father's stores, with a bright wrist-strap, and guaranteed to take perfect pictures every time.

Nick did not try to hide his amusement at the toy, and Judi's lips compressed as she snapped the zip shut.

'I'd forgotten I'd left it in my bag.'

She had not forgotten. She had worked out that, as Nick was taking professional shots, he would get the best angles on whatever views he aimed at, and while she was waiting for him to take them, she might be able unobtrusively to station herself nearby, and stun her friends with the results when she returned home.

She said grudgingly, 'I'll leave it behind, if you'd rather.'

'Bring it along, if you want to. You've got it to carry, not me. Add these to it.' He handed her a sturdy note-block and some ballpoint pens, and told her, 'We're heading for Lak Muang first. You might as well take down the gen about it before we start off. It'll give you some idea of what you'll be expected to do.'

'Lak Muang?' Her pronunciation was a passable imitation of his own, and earned Judi a keen look as she flipped open the note-block and got ready to take his dictation.

'L-a-k . . .' he spelled it out. 'Best to take down the Thai names in longhand. I don't want the bother of unravelling your interpretations from wads of notes afterwards.'

Judi was too busy keeping up with his dictation to retort. He shot his words out with the rapidity of machine-gun fire. 'Foundation-stone of city...traditional meeting-place...widely believed the stone has the power to grant wishes.'

Nick stretched her shorthand speed to the limit—deliberately, Judi felt sure, and was grateful for her habit of taking dictation from the radio now and then to sharpen her shorthand skills, which enabled her now to keep up with him, whereas a normal speed-writer would have been hopelessly left behind.

Her downbent gaze missed the gleam in the man's eyes as her pen sped over the surface of the paper, and stopped only two words behind him when he finished, remaining poised, waiting without apparent concern for him to go on.

'That'll do for now,' he said abruptly. 'When we get back, type each caption on a separate sheet of paper, in case I want to add on bits later.'

Did that exclude her from the coming dinner and floor-show this evening? Judi wondered, and knew that Pet would be only too delighted if it did, but pride refused to allow her to ask in case Nick might think she was begging his permission to go along as well.

He said, 'Let's go. We'll catch a taxi.'

Judi enquired with false meekness, 'Do you want me to carry anything?'

He flung her a straight look over his shoulder. 'No woman carries my gear.'

He made no bones about not trusting her with his precious equipment. Judi flashed, 'I only prang cars. I don't drop things.'

'It wouldn't matter too much if you did. Most of my gear is shock-proof. I just don't believe in women's lib; at least, not to that extent.'

Judi wondered to what extent this chauvinistic male did believe in it, and whether Nick himself was as shock-proof as he professed his gear to be. It would be playing a dangerous game to find out. She felt a tingle of excitement curl up her spine at the prospect. If she got bored with being his secretary, it might be fun to try.

She resisted an impish urge to walk a meek two steps behind him when he spun on his heel and began to walk towards the door, and discovered to her chagrin that she had no option; her own much shorter legs took long seconds, and an undignified trot, to catch up with him.

They emerged together, to be met by the usual babble of taxi-drivers touting for fares. One shouldered his way through the scrum with the confident smile of having been pre-booked.

He flung the door of his cab wide, and beckoned Judi to step inside. She felt Nick waiting to see if she would make a move, but the green-lined brim of her linen sun-hat shaded her face from his oblique glance, and she kept her eyes averted, refusing to meet his, pretending not to notice the taxi-man's invitation, and remaining instead glued to Nick's side, silently demonstrating to him her knowledge of Eastern habits, waiting for him to haggle over the fare first.

She listened, fascinated, while he did so. The bargaining was short and sharp, and Judi could not follow what was being said because Nick spoke rapidly in fluent Thai, a disadvantage from the taxi-driver's point of view, since he could not claim to misunderstand.

The man's smile did not waver, however, and at the conclusion of the argument he took his seat behind the wheel with an alacrity that showed he was satisfied with the fare being offered.

Nick told Judi, 'You can get in, now.'

She was already on her way. She ducked into the dim interior, which even at this early hour was already hot, and felt her skin prickle with the humidity.

Its discomfort increased as the photographer slid in beside her, and Judi caught her breath. Nick sitting on the other side of a meal table was one thing, she discovered, but at close quarters in the cramped confines of a taxi it was altogether different.

And totally unnerving.

The taxi-driver catapulted his vehicle into the stream of traffic, swung round a corner without slackening speed, and hurled his two passengers together with the happy abandon of two dice being rattled round an eggcup. Judi grabbed for a hold as she slid helplessly to the edge of the seat, and wailed, 'The drivers here are worse than those in France.'

'You can't complain. Your own driving defies description.'

The first time they had met, Nick had described her driving without difficulty, and the memory still stung, but Judi's sharp retort expired in a gasp as his arms came round her just as she was about to fall on to the cab floor.

'That's what is called being in the Nick of time,' he quipped, and she laughed nervously.

He lifted her back on to the seat as if she had no more weight than a child, but he did not completely release her. He kept one arm across her, like a living seat-belt, and Judi shivered involuntarily at the contact.

Nick's arm, bared above the elbow by the high rolled sleeve of his khaki bush shirt, lay tanned and sinewy across her lap, a fine down of tawny hair highlighting the deep bronze of his skin.

The feel of it was like having a live electric wire across her lap. It sent out impulses that burned worse than the curry had done the night before, and gave a whole new depth of meaning to Nick's warning, 'Stick to what you can handle.'

Judi shifted uneasily in her seat, and hastily reversed her decision to try to shock this man. The shocks she was receiving now were already more than she could handle, and if he did not move his arm away soon she feared that the burn it left behind might not be so easily eradicated as the one she had received from the curry.

With difficulty she dragged her eyes away from his arm, and discovered her mistake when they rested instead on the wide open neck of his shirt, unbuttoned half-way to his waist against the growing heat of the day, and tantalisingly revealing a fine-tuned torso that, unlike Pet's, carried not a single surplus ounce.

Her pulses began to hammer, and she thought raggedly, It might have been better if Pet had come along with us, after all. She both wished she had and felt glad she had not, and grasped gratefully at the driver's comprehensive, 'Here!' to release her from sensations that were rapidly getting out of control.

Nick removed his arm from across her, and left behind a jumble of relief and bereavement as mixed as Thai curry. He paid off the driver, and told Judi crisply, 'You've already taken down the description for this shot, so you might as well spend the time posing for me. That green and white dress and hat you're wearing will be the perfect foil for the costumes of the dancers.'

He was honest enough to admit that it was her dress, and not herself, that he wanted in his picture, and pique and interest warred in Judi as he approached the waiting dancing troupe. More coins changed hands, and only interest remained as the girls began to dance.

Judi forgot her pique, and almost, but not quite, managed to forget Nick himself as she stared, entranced, at the exquisite grace of the young performers. Their vivid costumes floated to the dip and sway of the rhythm, moulding their lissom bodies that moved with a fluid grace, beautiful to watch.

Judi thought, If I miss the floor-show tonight, I don't care. This dancing, in the open air, under a cobalt sky, must surely surpass anything performed indoors.

Nick intruded into her thoughts with a crisp, 'Get out your own camera, and take a picture of them.'

Judi jerked back to awareness of him. 'You mean, you don't mind?'

'I don't care whether you actually take a shot or not. If you don't want a picture of the dancers, just pretend to take one. I want a picture of you, pointing your camera at them.'

Herself this time, not her dress. Judi experienced a curious thrill of pleasure, but before she could savour it Nick killed it with a brutal, 'It's a good idea to get someone who is an obvious tourist in one or two of the brochure shots, just to show would-be customers that they can snap the same things with their own box Brownies.'

His scorn slated her choice of camera, and a sharp retort rose to Judi's lips, but before it could surface he compounded his offence with, 'You look like a typical tourist. The classic English miss, in her so-correct dress and hat. Your mouth was almost as wide open as your eyes, watching the girls dance.'

The villain! Judi shot him a furious look. 'What did you expect me to come in? A bikini?' Hurriedly she ducked the answer that threatened in the gleam of his eyes, and rushed on, 'I'm not here to pose for your photographs. I was engaged as your secretary, not as a model.'

'You were engaged as a member of my team, and we all pull together. You will either co-operate, or get lost,' he told her curtly, and Judi flushed.

The last thing she wanted was to lose the job just as she had started it, but a covert look at Nick's hard face told her he meant exactly what he said, and did not care either way.

She swallowed, counted ten, and forced out, 'Where do you want me to stand?'

She hated the quick triumph in his look as he answered, 'Over there, in front of the vendor with the birdcages. He'll make a bit of background interest. That's far enough,' as Judi backed a few steps. 'Now, half turn towards me . . .'

The next quarter of an hour was a time of torture for Judi. Nick took endless minutes on each shot, not satisfied until he had got every angle exactly to his liking.

His voice rasped her, 'Hold your camera higher. Don't point it so much towards me. More in the direction of the dancers,' and so on, until she felt ready to scream.

The heat increased until it seemed as if she were standing in the middle of a blast furnace. Perspiration trickled down her face, but when she raised her hand to wipe it away Nick called out sharply, 'Don't move. You'll spoil my shot.'

People stopped to stare. A group of tourists discussed Judi openly, making no effort to lower their voices.

'Perhaps she's a cover-girl,' one hazarded, and another answered with a snigger, 'Shouldn't think so. She's got too many clothes on for Page Three.'

They walked away, laughing among themselves, and Judi squirmed with embarrassment. Nick's camera lens leered at her like a prying eye, an extension of Nick's own eye behind the viewfinder, probing into her very thoughts. She wriggled under the surveillance, and saw him smile, a brief, sardonic twisting of his lips that saw her discomfiture, and mocked it.

Frantic twitters rose from the captives in the bamboo birdcages stacked behind her, adding to her distress, and when Nick called out, 'For goodness' sake, try to look a bit happier. You're supposed to be a tourist enjoying yourself,' Judi's patience snapped.

'How can I feel happy when I'm standing right by these poor little creatures?' She threw an anguished look at the birdcages, and her voice ground to a halt.

Instantly Nick lowered his camera, and strode to join her. 'Release one, if that will put a smile on your face.'

'Release one?' She stared at him, not understanding.

'That's what they're being sold for, to be released.' He delved into his pocket again, and exchanged a coin for a cage, and explained the contradiction as he rested it in her outstretched arms.

'People believe they gain merit if they release a bird. Which means the vendor has a steady stream of customers, which gives him a good living, and the birds don't remain captive for long. When you release one here, at the city stone, it's customary to make a wish as well. Don't you remember the caption I dictated to you, before we set out?'

Judi nodded. 'I don't believe in the wish bit, but I'll be glad to set the bird free.'

'Take the peg out of the cage door, like this.' Nick demonstrated, and added, 'Don't do it until I tell you.' He backed away from her, camera at the ready. 'Now!' he called when he was suitably distant, and obediently Judi pulled out the peg, the light bamboo door fell open, and the twittering captive hopped to the edge of the cage and fluttered free.

Involuntarily Judi raised her face to watch it fly up into the sunshine, smiling at the joy of its freedom. Her heart rose with the little ex-prisoner and, in spite of her denial, somewhere deep inside her there rose as well a half-unconscious wish, to fly with the bird.

She closed her mind against what it revealed, and schooled her face to hide her feelings as Nick came back and took the empty cage from her, handed it back to the vendor, and said, 'That was great. It should make a super shot. Now, let's go somewhere cooler, before you melt.'

'How inconvenient for you if I did,' Judi bit back.

Nick laughed, and took her by the arm, and said, 'Wipe your face dry, and come and have a drink before we start again.'

Judi felt as if she had already been on the move for hours, and was surprised when she glanced at her watch to discover that it was still only mid-morning. She used the excuse of fumbling for her handkerchief to wipe her face, in order to free herself from Nick's hold on her elbow, which spread a paralysing tingle through her arm that threatened to render her muscles useless.

'In here,' Nick guided her, and she walked beside him into cool dimness, under revolving ceiling fans that sent a welcome current of air across the restaurant tables.

Judi excused herself and escaped to the powder-room, where she laved her face and arms in blissfully cool, scented water, and felt more in command of herself when she returned to join Nick at the table. He had already ordered drinks for both of them.

Judi eyed the contents of her long glass with unconcealed suspicion, and Nick read her expression with amusement.

'That won't burn your mouth.'

'It isn't funny to play tricks with someone else's food and drink.'

His face tightened, and he threw her accusation right back at her. 'The curry last night was no trick. You ordered it yourself. Dave warned you.'

And in a fit of bravado she had ignored the warning, and paid the price. Was she about to pay a surcharge now? Still hesitant, she raised the glass to her lips, and Nick said, 'It's pure fruit juice. Nothing else. It won't burn, I promise you. And it doesn't carry a punch.'

Curiously, Judi believed him, even before she sipped at the sweet, refreshing liquid, which brought back renewed strength as it slipped down her parched throat. She leaned back in her chair and admitted, 'It's good.'

'Drink lots, until you get used to the heat.'

'I *am* used to the heat. I told you . . .'

Nick taunted, 'An annual holiday on the Costa, and a once-in-a-lifetime visit to India?'

The man's guesswork was uncannily accurate. Judi gave him a startled look and blurted, 'How did you know?'

He grinned. 'I didn't.' And Judi could have kicked herself for so easily falling into his trap.

He continued, 'You need to live in a climate to really get used to it.'

'Every little must help,' she returned defensively.

'Exactly why I used you in my photographs,' he answered, pan-faced. Judi's eyes flew up and met a teasing twinkle in his, mocking her diminutive stature, but without malice. She joined in his laughter, and felt better as they finished their drinks and left the restaurant together with a rapport she would not have believed possible half an hour ago.

It made her more willing to co-operate when he placed her in front of his camera, taking shots of a temple, soon afterwards. She even found it fun pretending to be a tourist, and her smile was unforced this time as she faced the lens, and became brighter still when Nick applauded, 'You're learning fast.'

It faded slightly when she reflected upon what she was learning—about this disturbing stranger who was now her boss, and, more disturbing still, about her own reactions to him.

She was vividly aware of him close beside her as they paced a tranquil temple courtyard, an oasis of peace after the noise and bustle of the streets they had just left, its silence enhanced rather than broken by the background tinkle of bells, rung by the light breeze.

They paused for Nick to take a quick snapshot as a flock of pigeons suddenly took to the air and wheeled above them in a pale cloud. Judi, watching them, murmured, 'Except for the sunshine, we might be standing in Trafalgar Square.'

'Even to the lions,' Nick agreed gravely, and turned her to look at a ferocious, sculpted beast standing guard nearby. 'He's supposed to frighten off evil spirits.'

According to Dave, Nick bore the lion sign. It was reflected in his autocratic manner, his tawny colouring, and the charisma that acted like a magnet to attract hidden depths within herself which she had never suspected before, and which frightened her more than the prospect of any lurking spirits. She was in difficulty enough already, without inviting any more problems.

The temple rose above them in many tiers, its gilded tiles shimmering in the bright sunlight. The flyaway roof, resting on top like the decoration on some exotic wedding cake, reminded her of the nature of her troubles, which would still be waiting to be resolved when she returned home.

'Are we allowed inside the temple?' She shook away the reminder, and Nick answered,

'Yes, but you must take off your shoes first.'

The sweet, sickly smell of incense hung heavy on the air, and Judi shivered as they padded barefoot across the cool floor tiles, and could not make up her mind whether it was from the contrast with the steamy heat outside or the disquieting contact of Nick's hand on her bare arm as he drew her to a standstill beside him, the better to appreciate the immense statue of the Buddha, smiling down at them in silent benevolence, the author of the gentle philosophy that was mirrored in the smiling faces of the people of this lovely land.

Outside again they put on their shoes, and Nick dictated a potted history of the temple, and told Judi, 'That's enough for your first day. It'll run you in nicely for a visit to the markets tomorrow.'

'You make me sound like a reconditioned car engine.'

Nick gave a throaty laugh, and destroyed their short-lived rapport with his riposte, 'Any engine that had you at the helm would need a lot of reconditioning.'

Judi's lips tightened. 'You needn't feel obliged to run me in. I'm not a tender plant that needs coddling.'

'I'm not coddling you. I want all those captions typed up, and some of my own hand-written notes copied out as well. You'll have plenty to keep you occupied when we get back to the hotel.'

The sight of his broad shoulders leading the way along the corridor to the room designated as a workroom for the team occupied Judi's mind in a distracting fashion when the taxi decanted them back at the hotel.

'Order yourself some lunch,' Nick told her. 'I'm having a working-lunch in my room. I'll show you where your equipment is, and leave you to get on with it.'

The room was equipped with a couple of tables, on one of which Nick dumped his photographic equipment; on the other reposed a typewriter not unlike the electric machine Judi was accustomed to using at the language school.

Nick said, 'Anything you can't understand, ask me about later. I'll be busy for the next few hours.'

Which meant, don't disturb her boss. Underlining the subservient nature of her position. Judi lowered her eyes to the wad of hand-written papers which Nick had given her to type, and assured him stiffly, 'I won't disturb you at all, if I can help it.'

A half-second later, she was startled to feel his fingers come up under her chin, forcing her to look up at him again.

'That's the understatement of the year,' he said, and added something in Thai which she did not understand, but the tone in which he said it was deep and provocative, and accompanied by a curving of the well-cut lips that brought hot colour rushing to her cheeks.

'You would disturb any man worth his salt, from nine years old to ninety, Judi,' he told her softly, and his hair made a tawny mane that blotted out the room as he bent his head and pressed his lips down on to her startled mouth before it could frame a reply.

CHAPTER THREE

JUDI'S lips burned from a fire hotter than any curry. She raised shaking hands to her face as Nick released her, and his low laugh taunted her as he strode through the communicating door into his own room, and shut it behind him.

Judi sank limply on to the chair behind the typewriter. In vain she lashed herself, 'Anyone would think you'd never been kissed before.'

She had been kissed, many times, by other suitors before Robert. So why should Nick's single salutation have such a devastating affect upon her now?

She had coped with previous suitors, even Robert, but after one kiss from Nick she was finding it difficult to cope with herself.

Impatiently she rubbed the back of her hand across her mouth, trying to erase the bruising numbness that his lips had left behind. She started violently when the communicating door suddenly opened again, and Nick reappeared, carrying a brown manila folder in his hand.

Hastily Judi snatched her hand away from her face, but not before Nick's quick eyes had caught the movement; his glance mocked her, but all he said was, 'When you've typed up the papers, clip them to the others in the folder.'

He put it down on the table and disappeared again, leaving her red-faced and fumbling, with a longing to hurl the folder after his retreating back.

With an immense effort Judi managed to resist the impulse. If she succumbed, she would only have to kneel down and pick up the papers from the floor, and her pride revolted at the possibility of Nick coming back through the door again to find her kneeling in front of him.

No doubt it would cause him considerable amusement, but she was not employed as his jester, and with a tight face she forced herself back to the table, and settled behind the typewriter.

Settled was a misnomer. Her jangled nerves made no sense of the bold handwriting that covered the wad of papers in tightly packed lines, and destroyed any hope she might have of concentrating on the contents.

Her pulses hammered, echoing the jerky rhythm of the typewriter keys as she flung herself into transposing the almost copperplate script into characterless print, striving desperately to restore a measure of calm to her shaken nerves.

She went rigid when a knock sounded on the door from the corridor outside, but her tense, 'Come in,' revealed only a waiter pushing a small trolley in front of him, and she thought, how silly—Nick wouldn't knock.

She stared at the trolley. She had not ordered any lunch for herself. Her scattered wits had not yet latched on to mundane needs, and her tightly knotted stomach revolted at the mere thought of food.

She began, 'Have you come to the right room?' when the waiter enlightened her.

'Professor Compton, he order for you.' He removed the covering napkins with a flourish before taking his broad smile back through the door again.

Judi investigated the offering with disfavour. Sandwiches. Fruit. And a large pot of strong coffee. Did Nick think she needed a restorative after his kiss? The pot stood on its tray like a silent taunt, and the urge to fling things returned.

Her hands tightened into fists, and her convulsive movement caught them against the typewriter keys. The electronics gave a protesting buzz, reminding her that she still had work to do. Perhaps the coffee might help, after all.

She cast an apprehensive glance at the communicating door, but it remained shut, and after a few seconds' hesitation she poured out a dark, aromatic cupful and, contrary to her usual practice, added a liberal lacing of sugar.

The strong, sweet drink steadied her, and she tried a sandwich, and discovered that she was hungry. Selecting another, she set her modest repast on the table beside her, and started to work.

To her surprise, Judi soon became absorbed in the content of the pages. The concise wording proved Dave's description of Nick as an authority on the country, and held her interest so completely that she did not notice the passing of time.

Her fingers flew over the typewriter keys, eager to keep pace with her eyes as they devoured a mixture of legend and travelogue that held her fascinated until the very last word.

Such was the force of Nick's narrative that she turned to tap the pile of typewritten sheets beside her into order, before adding the last one on top, feeling as if she had just returned from a long journey.

Nick could not fault her presentation of it either, she decided with justifiable pride. Although the typed pages lacked the character of his bold handwriting, the neat result had an attraction of its own.

She bent over the stack to realign one sheet which insisted upon poking out at an angle to its fellows, and a heavy lock of hair fell across her eyes, blocking her vision. With both hands occupied, Judi tossed her head to get it out of her way, but immediately she bent over her work again it swung back to its former position, irritatingly just across the very spot where she most wanted to look.

She gave an impatient exclamation, but before she could toss it back again it lifted out of her way of its own accord, and stayed there meekly, allowing her uninterrupted vision.

There was no draught in the room sufficient to move her hair. Efficient air-conditioning made fans unnecessary, so what...? Startled, she looked up, straight into Nick's face.

'I...you...I didn't see you come in,' she stammered.

She had not heard him, either, but that was not surprising. His lithe stride was as noiseless as that of a cat, and it would take radar sensitivity to pick up the sound of his footfalls on the smooth floor.

How long had he been standing there, watching her?

His fingers played idly with the strands of hair he had moved away from her face, making a silky link between them, and Judi felt her scalp tingle as he wound the shining length round his fingers, making experimental waves.

Waves of a completely different kind ebbed and flowed between them, beating at the door of her senses. Hastily Judi stirred into action, for fear they might break down the door, and submerge her as they rushed through. With a swift tug she pulled the last sheet of typing paper from the machine, in her confusion forgetting to release the grips that held the paper in place.

The brutal ejection rolled the platen round at unaccustomed speed, and forced from it a harsh, rasping sound as it gave up the captive sheet of paper. The mechanical protest cut the tension of silence between them, and Nick let her hair fall, and said, 'I'll take the papers.'

'I haven't checked the typing yet.'

Judi hugged the manila folder of papers like a shield between herself and Nick, and eyed him warily from behind them.

'I've got to read through them myself anyway, and there can't be any major errors. There weren't any at all on the last few sheets. I know, because I've stood here reading them while you've been typing.'

The last few sheets... How many were 'few'? It pointed to Nick standing behind her unnoticed for some time, watching her at work. Or simply watching her?

Uneasily, Judi was reminded of the silent patience of a cat, watching its prey, and the tingle that had started in her scalp inched downwards along her spine, touching her with icy fingers, so that she had to make a conscious effort to suppress a shiver.

Nick reached downwards, and instinctively she shrank back and checked herself just in time, deriding herself: don't be an idiot. He wants the papers, not you.

Slight though her movement was, Nick's quick eyes caught it and gave it his own interpretation; reading the flare of laughter in the gold eyes, Judi knew humiliatingly that his interpretation was word perfect, and he had scored over her yet again.

Tensely she began, 'If there are any corrections to be made, mark them and let me have the sheets back.'

'I'll drop them on the table by the typewriter when we go out to dinner tonight.'

'I'll have them done for you when you get back.'

An illogical wave of disappointment swept over Judi. That meant she would not be going to the restaurant with Nick, after all. She had no time to wonder at the intensity of her feeling of let-down, since she had already seen one dancing display that day, when Nick cut in, 'What makes you think you won't be coming?'

'You're going out to dinner, and a floor-show.'

'We're *all* going out to assess the floor-show, to see if it's worth taking the tour members to see, and the opinion of each member of the team now is valuable. We're here to work, not for personal pleasure.'

It was on the tip of Judi's tongue to retort, so long as you remember that, too, but one look at the dominant lines of Nick's face hovering uncomfortably close to her own decided her against it, and she remained silent as he went on, 'Wherever the team goes, you go too. I don't hire a secretary and then go to the trouble of carting a tape-recorder round with me.'

In other words, he did not hire a dog and bark himself. Nick was a master at the art of putting people down, and resentment flared inside Judi, as much at the ease with which he seemed able to yo-yo her emotions between one extreme and the other as at his autocratic manner.

She returned stiffly, 'What time am I supposed to be ready to go out?'

'Why ask me, when Pet said seven o'clock?'

Pet had said nothing of the kind in Judi's hearing, but if she started an argument on the subject now it would probably spill over into the evening, and with Pet present the atmosphere was likely to be strained enough as it was.

Biting back a sharp retort, Judi asked, 'Do you want me to do anything else for you before then?'

'That, Judi, is a leading question. But if you mean typing, the answer's no.'

The look he slanted at her drew hot colour to Judi's cheeks, and he deepened it still further as he reached down and scooped up the manila folder full of papers, and she felt something light as a zephyr brush across the top of her hair that turned the tingles into an electric shock of pain, before Nick straightened, and his straying lips curved, mocking her confusion, while he instructed, 'Just remember to tuck a note-pad and pen in your evening-bag, and,' he reached the door to the corridor, wrenched it open and turned back to face her, so that he did not see behind him in the corridor, as Judi could, a flash of aggressively blonde hair, and a brightly printed cotton dress straining at the seams, as its owner paused on catching sight of him, 'and come looking pretty,' he finished provocatively, and closed the door on Judi's gasp.

But not before she had time to catch the look of rage on Pet's face, that boded ill for the peace of the coming evening out.

The first salvo was fired soon after they walked into the restaurant, less than two hours later. The proprietor welcomed them at the door, plainly eager to win their approval of his establishment, and reap the benefit of the tourist trade that would follow in their wake.

He placed his hands together in the gentle Thai greeting to Nick, instinctively recognising the tall, aristocratic figure as the head of the team. His action was not lost upon Pet, who smirked as if she personally had produced Nick out of a hat. As if she owned him, or at least had a prior claim on him, Judi thought disgustedly.

Nick returned the *wai* with a natural grace that did not look at all out of place with his Westernised appearance, and Judi thought, he fits in wherever he happens to be, just like a chameleon, and could not decide whether it was a trait she envied or felt suspicious of.

Pet returned the *wai* too, but her action looked clumsy and contrived, as if she were trying to force herself into a picture in which she did not quite fit, like the wrong piece of a jigsaw puzzle.

Unsure of what she ought to do, Judi contented herself with a smile, and asked Dave in an aside as they walked into the cool dimness of the restaurant, under slowly revolving fans, 'Should I have returned the *wai*? I wasn't sure what to do.'

'Best not——' Dave began.

Then Nick cut in, 'If you're not sure what to do in Thailand, just smile,' and added with a smile of his own, 'Yours should get you by in any country.'

His unexpected smile made Judi feel warm inside, but it seemed to have the effect of raising Pet's temperature to simmering point. She snapped, 'Outsiders don't understand these things. There are degrees of height for the hands in a *wai*, according to the person you're greeting. If you tried, and did it wrong, you'd cause offence.'

That puts me in my place, Judi thought with tightened lips, and the silent reservation that Pet could cause offence without even trying. She tucked herself in beside Dave as the proprietor led them to a low table positioned so that they would have an uninterrupted view of the floor-show while they ate.

The table-top was so close to the floor that it reminded Judi of Japanese-style eating habits, and the cushions placed round it as seats confirmed the likeness. She frowned. There were only three cushions.

Nick noticed the number at the same time. 'We shall need another cushion,' he told the proprietor. 'We are four, not three.'

'Another one shall be brought right away.' The man's smile became slightly fixed as he gave an order to a hovering waiter, and then turned back to Nick. 'Miss Welsh, she only order a meal for three.'

Pet had done this to embarrass her, Judi felt convinced, and her suspicion was confirmed by the sly look of malice which the other woman sent in her direction, while she excused her omission offhandedly with, 'I forgot we'd got an odd one tagging along with us.'

As if Judi was some kind of unwanted appendage, she fumed, and not a part of the team. She drew in a sharp breath to retort, but Nick got in first with a curt, 'Be sure not to make the same mistake when you're arranging a tour for clients. A member of the team doesn't matter.'

Did he mean to stress that she was a member of the team, or that she did not matter? Judi did not know whether to feel pleased or deflated as Nick finished with a warning to Pet, 'A company guest might not be charitable. After paying out a fortune they deserve to have all the arrangements run smoothly on a tour.'

Pet gave a tight smile. 'I've been doing this for too long to make that kind of mistake,' she assured him confidently, and confirmed that this time was no mistake.

Pet had won, and lost, Judi reflected, as well as earning herself a rebuke from Nick; so round one was about evenly matched. She smiled her thanks to the waiter who provided her with the extra cushion, and taking her cue from Nick she sank gracefully down on to its soft comfort, tucking her legs underneath her with the neatness of a kitten.

Her years of energetic workouts at the local gym had given her a lissom suppleness that held her slender body as erect as the stem of a flower, and absorbed this novel method of sitting at a table without the slightest discomfort.

Pet was obliged to lower her much greater bulk in awkward stages, and held herself into as near an upright position as she could manage, by using her one hand and arm as a prop, presenting an inelegant contrast that her vitriolic look at Judi said was not lost upon her.

Automatically the four adopted the same seating arrangement that they used at the hotel, which left Pet sitting next to Nick, and Dave and Judi together, with Judi opposite to Nick.

Almost, she wished she had been sitting beside him so that she would not have to look at him. He was startlingly handsome in his formal tropical whites; they had the effect of darkening his tan, and making his tawny-coloured hair stand out in greater contrast.

Her eyes seemed to find it an irresistible magnet, and each time they looked up, his seemed to be resting on her with a disconcerting gleam in them that registered the confusion they were causing, and enjoyed the power to create it.

In desperation Judi dragged her gaze away and looked at her surroundings, trying to avoid Nick's look. In spite of the traditional Thai décor, the cuisine was international, and she ducked the challenge in Nick's stare that dared her to try curry again, and cautiously ordered French instead. She found it flat and uninteresting by comparison, as was the floor-show that followed, although it drew enthusiastic applause from the rest of the packed diners.

Judi clapped, but half-heartedly, and wondered, what on earth is the matter with me? Everybody else loved it. She did not know how to answer when Nick asked of the table in general, when the show was over, 'What do you think of it as an attraction for one of the tours?'

Pet had already made her opinion of the show perfectly clear, and she could not hide her vexation that Nick should defer to the opinion of the others—particularly, Judi suspected, her own.

Dave enthused, 'Fine. It's just the job. The tourists will love it, particularly all this authentic Thai décor.'

Nick pressed, 'Judi?'

She must either co-operate, or get lost. She did not want to answer, but she did not want the alternative either, and caught between the two impossibles she picked up her wineglass and sipped thoughtfully in order to give herself time to think.

How was she to answer? The floor-show was excellent. The dancing equalled that which she had watched earlier in the day. But Nick's eyes were fixed on her face, reading her lack of enthusiasm, just as he would read between the lines if she tried to pass off his question with a non-committal reply.

But, if she told him that she found the floor-show lack-lustre, what reason could she give for her opinion? Was the lack in the show, or in herself? The question tracked across her mind unheralded and, startled, her hand tightened on the fragile glass, threatening its slender stem.

Why had the zest gone from the food, and the dancing, for her? Urgently she tried to tell herself that it was because she had seen the other dancing in the open air, gilded by the bright sunshine. Without much success, she tried to suppress the thought that it might be because then she'd been on her own with Nick.

The thought brought back his warning with renewed force, 'Don't take on anything you can't handle.'

Judi surveyed him across the rim of her wineglass, and his impatient expression warned her that he was not prepared to wait forever for her reply. She took another sip to boost her courage, and decided on the simple truth. That way, Nick would not be able to catch her out afterwards.

'The food can't be faulted.' Her voice was level, defending her right to eat French instead of Thai if she wished. 'But I think the display of dancing we watched this morning was much better. The floor-show was good, but somehow it seemed to lack that extra edge. Perhaps the open-air dancing scored from its surroundings. They gave it added atmosphere.'

Judi had not meant to imply that she and Nick had stood together to watch the dancing that morning, but some imp linked the words together, so that they came out sounding that way.

In fact, Nick had watched the display only through his viewfinder, and placed Judi some distance away from him as part of the general landscape for his shot, but Pet took the words at their face value, and must have made the imp smile at its success as she cut across Nick's thoughtful, 'That's a point to be considered,' with a waspish,

'What do you know about what tourists will or won't want? This sort of research is best left to professionals.'

Judi sent the older woman an exasperated look. Pettish would be a more appropriate name for her, she thought, irritated. The woman really was impossible. If she wanted Nick, she was more than welcome to him, and she felt strongly tempted to tell Pet so there and then, and clear the decks of any misunderstanding, so that the rest of the tour could go ahead in peace.

But, if Pet was determined to pick a fight, Judi did not intend to leave herself undefended. She retorted, 'Surely the tourists themselves have the final choice? They must, if you want their custom a second time round. I assume that's what you're aiming at, since the tourists are your bread and butter?'

So much for Pet's scornful air of superiority. Judi hit back hard, but did not care. Pet had asked for it, and, if she discovered that her opponent would retaliate, perhaps she would be less inclined to fight. Judi went on relentlessly, 'As a professional, you've got an axe to grind in bringing tourists to these places. I haven't. I look at things from the same point of view as your clients, which must make my opinion more valuable than yours.' She ignored a smothered snort from Dave beside her, and added deliberately, 'Nick says I'm a typical tourist,' as if it had been a compliment, instead of just the opposite.

The tight lines about Pet's mouth, which even her heavy make-up could not disguise, told Judi that her shot had gone home, but, undeterred, Pet thrust back, 'Tourists can't tramp the streets forever. They've got to sit down some time, and they want entertainment while they eat.'

'But perhaps not sitting down on cushions?' Judi suggested. 'I imagine most of your clients are getting on in years, otherwise they wouldn't be able to afford your astronomical prices, and they'll have the same difficulty in getting down to floor level, not to say balancing while they eat.'

She did not say, the same difficulty *as you*, but Pet's reddening face told Judi that she had not misunderstood, and she thought with swift shame, I needn't have been so bitchy.

It went against her normally friendly nature. Perhaps that nature had acquired a tougher outer casing since she had been so badly used herself by Robert and her own family. Before Pet could reply, however, Dave cut across the hostile crossfire with a placatory, 'Why not put it in the brochure as an alternative to a hotel dinner, and leave the clients to choose for themselves?'

The man was a diplomat, Judi thought drily, and felt relief when Dave proved himself again by adding, 'If you're going to walk back to the hotel, Nick, we'd better be going. The sky is starting to look ominous.'

High-banked clouds had crept unnoticed over the sky while they were eating, symptomatic of the atmosphere between the team, that was a team in name only, Judi decided, as Pet exclaimed, '*Walk* back? But, I thought . . .'

'You can go back by taxi, if you'd rather,' said Nick. 'I want to get some shots of the city by night.'

Typically the photographer had brought his camera along with him. It remained always at his side, like a third arm. Just as he expected her to tote along her notebook and pen, Judi thought. Nick looked across at her as if he could read what was going on in her mind, and said, 'I hope you can manage to take down dictation in the dark, while you're walking.'

Which meant that he expected Judi to walk back with him. His words instantly made up Pet's mind for her.

'If you're going to walk, I will, too,' she decided.

Judi hoped for Pet's sake that the older woman had managed to snatch the rest during the day which Nick had suggested to her earlier. It was a good three miles back to the hotel, probably more if Nick took photographic diversions; and, once committed to Shanks' pony, for safety's sake Pet would be obliged to remain with the party, and walk the whole distance. However, that was Pet's problem. Judi gave a mental shrug, and answered Nick.

'I don't need light to take notes. I can thumb-space the lines on my pad,' she announced confidently, as if she was used to taking down shorthand in the dark, on her feet, every day of her life.

Pet grumbled, 'If you had said we'd be walking back, I'd have brought a jacket along with me.'

She gave a significant glance at Nick, as if she hoped he might proffer his own, but before Nick could respond Dave cut in with an uncharacteristically tactless, 'My jacket would fit you better, if you're feeling cold.'

Judi had to hide a grin as Pet snapped, 'I'm not. But it gets chilly if it showers.'

Pet had brought a light wrap with her that should be quite sufficient to counteract any chill, Judi suspected, even if the clouds did erupt. She herself had brought a cashmere shawl which she had bought while she was in India. Its lace-like daintiness crushed up to almost nothing in her hands, but it was deliciously warm when she draped it across her shoulders.

Nick said, 'If you're all walking, let's go,' and flowed to his feet in one fluid movement.

Judi did the same, not needing Dave's outstretched hand to help her up, so he extended it to Pet instead, and hauled her to her feet, keeping her hand firmly tucked in his own so that she was obliged to stand by and watch as Nick turned to help Judi adjust the shawl over her shoulders, while telling her to, 'Walk with me, so that I can dictate to you as I go along.'

It left Pet with no option but to walk with Dave. Judi noticed that the older man retained a firm hold on his companion's hand and, glancing at his face, she surprised a satisfied look there, and sensed with quick intuition, Dave's in love with Pet.

Another triangle, she thought, suddenly depressed. Dave wanting Pet, and Pet wanting Nick, and... It was a mirror of herself and Robert, only the third point to their particular triangle had been purely financial, which made it less forgivable.

She gave a sigh, and hid it in the business of bending to unzip her bag to remove the notepad and pen, and asked Nick in a muffled voice, with her face averted,

'Don't you want to dictate the blurb about the restaurant now?'

'Not here. It looks too obvious. The proprietor would want to know what I was writing. If I refused to tell him, he would think it was adverse comment, and if I showed it to him, and it did not appear in the brochure later on, for lack of space or some other reason, he would wonder why. It's better to do it when we get back to the hotel.'

Judi nodded, and grabbed at her shawl which had slipped as she'd straightened up. She missed, but Nick's hand came down on her shoulder and prevented it from falling to the floor, and she gasped as she felt his hand come into contact with her skin.

The material of the shawl was gossamer fine, and it felt as if there was nothing between her bare shoulder and the palm of his hand. The effect was electric, and Judi knew an irrational urge to check to see if the heat of his touch had scorched the finely worked wool of her shawl. A faraway rumble drew an exclamation from Dave. 'That was thunder.'

Judi thought raggedly, I've already been struck by lightning.

She slung her bag over her shoulder to leave both her hands free for when Nick wanted to dictate, and, gripping her notebook and pencil like lifebuoys to keep her afloat, she hurried after Dave and Pet as they made their way to the door.

Nick remained behind for a few words with the proprietor of the restaurant. From a glance at the man's face, Judi sensed that he was being thanked for the meal and the entertainment, with the almost olde worlde courtesy that seemed to be an integral part of Nick, even although she could not understand what was being said, since the latter offered the added compliment of speaking in the proprietor's own language.

Nick caught up with them at the door, and Dave looked up at the sky and deduced, 'I reckon we'll make it. The storm seems to be some distance away yet.'

Nick nodded absently, as if the prospect of a wetting did not particularly bother him, so long as he obtained the photographs he needed.

Outside the air-conditioned restaurant, the heat was oppressive, made worse by the hovering storm, and Nick asked Pet again, 'Are you sure you wouldn't prefer to change your mind, and take a taxi back?'

He did not include Judi in his offer, and she did not know whether to take it as a compliment to her greater powers of endurance, or as a callous lack of consideration on Nick's part that expected her to suffer the discomforts of the walk along with him.

Pet retorted ungraciously, 'I said I'll walk,' and Nick gave the slightest shrug of his broad shoulders, and without another word led the way at a pace that made no concession to the heat or to end-of-day weariness.

Pride, of the rather childish, 'I'll show him, and Pet' variety, forced Judi to keep up with his fast pace without complaint, even when he lengthened the already long walk by a couple of diversions in order to obtain shots which even Judi's unprofessional eye could see were exceptional, taking the usual from an unusual angle with the perceptive eye of an artist.

Once, he used Pet and Dave as silhouettes. 'Stand close together, and look out over the canal,' he bade them, adding to Dave, when they did not stand close enough for his liking, 'Put your arm round her. That's right. Now, hold it for a moment.'

As he focused to take his shot, an idea germinated in Judi's mind. Unwittingly, Nick was playing right into Dave's hands, and the older man complied with his team leader's directions with obvious relish.

There was no accounting for taste, she qualified with an inward grimace, watching Dave hug Pet to him, but she felt she owed the older man something for introducing her to this job, and thereby giving her extra time in which to decide on the new life she wanted for herself, when she rejected the old one on her return to England.

Cupid was notorious for eroding the confidence of those he pricked with his arrows, even such a worldly-wise traveller as Dave, and if she could help him to achieve the new life of his desire she would have paid him back something for doing the same for her.

Judi tucked the thought away in the back of her mind as they started to walk again, and concentrated on Nick's sporadic dictation, using whatever light became available as they walked past the windows of clubs and restaurants along the way in order to keep the lines of writing from running into one another.

The storm broke when they were within a few yards of their hotel.

They had all been so absorbed in placing themselves in strategic positions for Nick to obtain a particular shot he wanted that they had not noticed the clouds above them growing rapidly heavier.

The oppressive heat lay like a thick blanket above them, smothering the air so that it felt difficult to breathe, until with the suddenness of a zip-fastener being ripped open the clouds broke and dropped their contents in one vast sheet of water.

With one accord, each man grabbed a girl and ran for the shelter of the nearest doorway. Judi felt her feet leave the ground as Nick tucked her under his arm, and covered the distance in three long jumps.

A minute later, Dave and Pet disappeared into another doorway several feet away along the street, and Nick released Judi back on to her feet, but he kept one arm round her shoulder, drawing her close against him to avoid the spindrift of spray that ricocheted up from the ground.

Judi sucked in a difficult breath. Getting wet would have been the lesser of two evils for her. A shower and a change of clothes afterwards would have removed any after-effects of a soaking, but it would take more than a shower to get rid of the feeling of Nick's hard frame pressing against her side, and she could not change her skin, which prickled all over from his closeness.

A flash of lightning, followed by an ear-splitting blast of thunder, increased the downpour to a deluge, and Judi forgot her inhibitions and cowered against Nick. He looked down into her wide eyes, and raised one hand to gently draw her shawl across her head, a token gesture of shelter from the elements that was curiously comforting, as he teased, 'You look like a novice, in your shawl.'

Judi did not feel like a novice. She did not feel like anything which she could identify, because she had never known feelings like those she was experiencing now.

Sensations as elemental as the storm itself washed over her, in a wave that made the monsoon pale by comparison, and, frightened more by the storm inside her than the one which lashed the empty streets, Judi clung to Nick and trembled.

He felt the tremor, and hugged her closer to him, instantly making it worse. Misunderstanding the reason, he consoled, 'There's no need to be frightened. It'll all be over in a few minutes.'

Judi knew that the storm she most feared would not cease so obligingly as nature's tantrum, and trembled all the more for fear of she knew not what.

The storm ceased as suddenly as it had started, but the aftermath left them with a problem. The streets were by now awash with several inches of water, more than enough to cover their ankles if they should venture to wade through it.

And the hotel was on the opposite side of the road.

Dave and Pet joined them, and Dave said ruefully, 'We're both soaked. We couldn't move with your sort of speed, and we got caught before we reached the doorway, so we might as well paddle.'

Without more ado he stepped into the swirling flood, drawing Pet along with him, and Nick breathed, 'What a shot!' and swung up his camera to focus on the wading pair.

The lights of the hotel made long shadows in the glistening flood, and Judi marvelled, 'No one else will have a picture like this one.'

Nick's teeth flashed white in his tanned face. 'It's a picture the travel firm won't want to publish in their brochure, that's for sure. Although the tours don't take place until the rainy season has ended, for obvious reasons.'

Judi exclaimed, 'I should think not! The drains can't cope with tons of water all at once, like that.'

'It's mostly the fault of the city fathers,' Nick answered. 'The most efficient drains they had were the canals. But with modern traffic, and an influx of tourists, the powers that be thought it would be a good idea to fill in a lot of the canals and turn them into roads, and now they are paying for their mistake. The storm water has got nowhere to drain into quickly, so they get floods instead, like this one.'

He slung his camera across his shoulder, and added, 'Come on. Let's go.'

'Can't we wait until it goes down a bit? We're not wet, and I don't fancy wading through that mixture of rubbish and water.'

Judi eyed the unsavoury flow with dubious eyes, and Nick said abruptly, 'It will take several hours to clear. I'm not waiting here for that long. And if you stand on your own in a doorway in Bangkok at this time of night, you will get yourself badly misunderstood.'

He turned derisive eyes on the mounting flush in Judi's cheeks as the meaning of his words penetrated, and added, 'But if you don't fancy the idea of paddling...'

He stooped swiftly and rolled up his trouser legs to the knee, and as he straightened up he caught Judi in his arms, swung her high and stepped out into the flood, carrying her safely above it.

It was too late to wish that she had followed Pet's example, and waded across. Nick held her firmly, too firmly for her to struggle free, even if she wanted to, and to her dismay an errant part of her did not, and it was not the muddy flood that was the cause of her reluctance.

The top of Judi's head rested just below Nick's chin, and her startled upwards look noted that it bore a small cleft in the point. An odd feeling shafted through her at the sight of it, made odder still by the acrobatic behaviour of her heart, which seemed to be trying to outpace the strong, even beats reaching her ear through the crisp white linen of his jacket.

Frozen into immobility in his arms, she could feel Pet's glare fixed on her from the hotel steps, where she and Dave turned to watch as Nick carried Judi safely across. Pet's face was a study as he mounted the step and set Judi down, neat and clean and dry against the older woman's sadly bedraggled appearance.

Nick told the two cheerfully, 'Cut along, both of you, and jump under a hot shower before you start to get the shivers.'

He kicked off his soaking sandals and, shaking them clear of water, dropped them into a nearby umbrella-stand to drain, before bending to return his trouser legs to their normal level. Then he strolled barefoot beside Judi, nodding with unshaken aplomb to groups of fellow hotel guests scattered about the lobby, who were pristine in unblemished evening dress.

Judi sent him an amused sideways glance. She could not help but admire the confidence that carried him through a situation which nine people out of ten would have found acutely embarrassing, herself included, and her amusement surfaced in a chuckle as they reached the room which Nick used as an office.

The soft, throaty sound brought his eyes swiftly down to rake her face. 'What's funny?'

'You are.' Her own eyes danced, and a gleam fired the depths of the golden ones looking back. 'Most people with bare, muddy feet would have skulked in by a back entrance, hoping to avoid being seen.'

'I'm not most people.'

That was the understatement of the year, Judi thought, and gave a gasp as Nick suddenly reached out and gripped her by the shoulders and pulled her towards him.

'The caption about the restaurant...' she stammered. 'You said you wanted to dictate it when we got back.'

'That can wait until the morning. I've got more important things to do right now.'

Whatever those things were, he seemed prepared to put them aside for the moment as well. He lowered his head, and claimed her mouth in a long, exploring kiss.

At the first touch of his lips, Judi's own parted, just as the storm clouds had parted, and the uprush of emotion that had so bewildered her in the shop doorway copied the rain, and poured through the gap in an uncontrollable flood.

Against her will, Judi's lips responded; feeling it, Nick's kiss changed, deepened, taking her mouth with a force that refused to be denied, and helplessly Judi knew that things for her would never be the same again.

The flood swept away the last fragile veils of her girlhood, and released the dormant womanhood that even being engaged to Robert had failed to bring into flower.

Nick's kiss provided the heat needed to draw the seed into life, and once it had burst from its hidden confines it must either flower or wither.

After a timeless age, Nick released her, and Judi stared up at him with dilated eyes.

His hair seemed to glow like a sun above her, reflecting the fire in his eyes, and she shrank from the fierce heat that threatened to consume her, scorching the life from the tender plant before it had time to grow and bloom.

CHAPTER FOUR

JUDI woke the next morning with a plan already formed in her mind. She would help Dave and herself at the same time.

Nick's kisses had got through to her the evening before with a disturbing force she could not have envisaged. He had said he could use her. But not in this way, she vowed.

Her own heightened sensitivity, and the newly awakened emotions aroused by the storm, must have left her more than usually vulnerable. It's being in the tropics, she excused herself. Or perhaps it was a rebound from Robert.

Whatever the reason, she recognised clearly that she was going to need an antidote to Nick's penetrating charisma, and quickly, if she hoped to return from her break in Thailand unscathed.

Her lips twisted at the irony of fleeing to Thailand to escape the consequences of one entanglement, and promptly getting herself involved in another. That it was only her own feelings which were disturbed, she did not doubt. Nick did not care either way. Men could kiss and run without the encounter leaving any lasting impression. But this time Nick had caught the wrong victim. She knew enough about herself now to be able to control whatever feelings assailed her, and she cared as little for Nick as he did for her.

Dave offered her a handy alternative.

She would flirt outrageously with the older man, she planned, and, if her behaviour made Pet jealous and awakened her to Dave's charms and what she was missing, so much the better. That part of it should be easy enough. Pet would be jealous of any man paying attention to any woman except herself, but if the ploy worked for Dave it would be worth the trouble, and hopefully it would serve to dilute the effect which Nick was having upon herself, at the same time.

His expert kissing had drawn deeply into the well of her emotions, the depths of which had never been so stirred before, and the transition from girl to awakened woman was swift and painful. She blamed Nick bitterly for adding that hurt to the bruising which she had already received from Robert.

When she opened her eyes on the new day, Judi knew that she was different from the girl who had awoken in the same bed the morning before. She *felt* different. More alive. More vibrant. Stronger. She would have no qualms now about giving Robert back his ring, or in facing her parents' wrath.

She swung her legs out of bed, and padded across to the dressing-table mirror. Did she look any different? The same wide eyes stared back at her, from the same small, heart-shaped face, still flushed with sleep, and attractively tanned now, in spite of her wearing a sun hat.

There was a subtle difference, though. Her eyes grew wider, trying to pinpoint it, and recognised the difference in themselves, without being able to define accurately exactly what it was they were looking at.

A glow shone in the velvet depths that had not been there before. It spread outwards, irradiating her face, and giving it a kind of bloom, like the bloom on a nearly ripened peach, she thought, bemused, and blushed at her own imagery, backing hastily away from the mirror before she was able to read any more.

In spite of her energetic efforts under a soapy shower, the bloom was still there when she returned to brush her hair into submission, and she hoped uneasily that Nick would not notice it, and guess the cause, when she went downstairs.

She would be a fool to deny his physical attraction, and an even greater fool to fall for it, but if the transition from girl to woman hurt, it could be made to work both ways. Nick would not find it so easy to sweep a woman away with his casual lovemaking as he would a girl.

I'm not that gullible any more, Judi assured herself, and walked downstairs with a confident spring in her step.

She came face to face with Nick in the doorway of the hotel dining-room, and discovered to her dismay that women were just as vulnerable as girls, when it came to men.

Increased awareness increased his attraction. Thank goodness it was only physical attraction, she consoled herself as he stood aside to allow her free passage, and she felt her heart perform its now familiar somersault as she slipped past him, accidentally brushing against his arm as he held the door wide.

She jinked away from the contact, and avoided the mocking glint in his eyes that derided her discomfort, and instead met Pet's cold stare from the table. The pale blue eyes passed on to Nick as he followed Judi into the room, and she felt a flash of pity as her own new recognition read naked hunger, mixed with desperation, in the older woman's look.

She thought with relief, no one can read that in mine. She had cause to be grateful to Robert, after all. Her engagement was all the reminder she needed of the pitfalls of getting entangled in another relationship. The next time, if there was to be one, she would take a long, cool look at the prospects, and commit herself only on her own terms.

Dave said without preamble when they sat down, 'I've asked Pet to help me sort out the travel arrangements for the up-country tour today. Can you spare her, Nick?'

'Sure, I can spare her,' Nick drawled, and seeing the suddenly stricken look on Pet's face Judi thought how cruel men could be.

She said aloud, 'How lovely,' with a lingering look in Dave's direction that envied Pet for being the one chosen to help him.

Her effort bounced off Dave's craggy features with no visible effect, and Judi thought ruefully, this is going to be harder than I bargained for. But Pet's sharp intake of breath told her that it had reached one target, at least.

Two, if she read Nick's scowl aright. He said abruptly, 'Judi's coming with me,' as if Dave had tried to claim her help as well. The older man nodded, unmoved.

'Pet and I can manage. We don't need anybody else.'

He might not, Judi thought, but Pet did, and was due for disappointment once again on what sounded as if it might be their last day in Bangkok, when Dave asked, 'Is it OK with you, Nick, if I book our own travel arrangements to Chiang Mai at the same time?

Will you be finished with the market shots today, or will you want another day to complete them?'

'Today will be enough.'

'What about our rooms here?'

'We'll retain them. It's easier than carrying all our gear round with us.'

That means I can leave my engagement ring in the hotel safe, Judi thought with relief, and promptly forgot the unwanted jewel as Pet grumbled, 'I can't understand why you want to take shots of Bangkok at all. The firm must already have lots on their file as it is.'

'But none of them taken by me,' Nick returned coolly, and Judi gasped.

How arrogant he was! How sure of himself, and the superiority of his own work above that of other people. Silence fell on the table; she toyed with her own modest slice of toast, and watched Pet demolish her cooked breakfast, but this time her disgust was tinged with understanding.

Perhaps misery was making Pet eat too much? Her own unhappiness had not so affected Judi, but she knew what it was like to feel that way.

Dave ate with his attention on scribbled notes covering the backs of several envelopes. He groaned, 'One of these days I'll get this mess sorted out.'

Judi put in quickly, 'Let me type out your notes for you,' as if she would regard it as a privilege.

'Later, if you've got any time left over from my typing,' Nick cut in. Then he drained his coffee-cup and ordered, 'It's time we were going.'

Showing who is the boss, Judi deduced, and sent Dave an apologetic smile that she hoped would register and start off her campaign on the right footing,

before she rose from her chair with what she hoped
was a convincing show of reluctance, to follow Nick
to the door.

Her reluctance failed to convince herself. She was
as eager to see the markets as any tourist, and to visit
them in the company of someone as knowledgeable
as Nick was an added bonus which not even the tour
operator's clients would enjoy.

She had longed to explore the markets while she'd
been in India, but each time she'd suggested the idea
Robert had always had a business contact whom he
simply must see while he was in the area, so that in
the end there had been no time for more than a small
amount of sightseeing, and that hurried. Now she intended to make up for lost opportunities.

She rejected the dress she'd worn yesterday. She did
not intend to give Nick the opportunity to sneer and
call her a typical tourist again. When she came downstairs, her fawn cotton slacks, rope-soled shoes and
fawn bush shirt in much the same pattern as his own,
but buttoned up higher to the neck, drew her an approving nod.

'You look workmanlike,' Nick commented, and
Judi felt an irrational flash of pleasure, which must
have shown in her expression because he added unexpectedly, 'Are you looking forward to it?'

'Our trip round the markets, you mean? Yes, im-
mensely.' She made her stand quite clear that it was
the markets, and not Nick's company, which she was
looking forward to, and his lips curved, acknowl-
edging her thrust.

'Of course, the markets,' he taunted, and watched
her colour rise before adding, 'So stop fighting, and

let's enjoy them together. There won't be time for another visit when we come back here.'

Judi felt grateful that Nick chose to walk, instead of taking a taxi. The truce eased the tension between them, and work provided a safe neutrality, still fragile enough to be destroyed by another such ride as they had endured yesterday.

Nick strolled, moderating his pace so that Judi was able to keep up with him easily. The early-morning streets were fresh, washed clean by the storm of the night before, and the air, as yet, was comparatively cool.

A saffron-robed monk squatted in the sunshine, his shaven head contrasting oddly with his youthful features, and his begging bowl set before him. Judi said impulsively, 'Wait a minute, while I give him something,' and delved into her bag for her purse.

For the first time in a long while she felt at peace with the world, and she vaguely wanted to thank somebody. The monk would do nicely.

She fished out a coin, but before she could offer it Nick's hand shot out and closed round her own, removing it from her fingers. 'I'll take it,' he said, and handed it to the man himself.

'Well, I like that!' Judi exploded. 'If you wanted to give him something, why didn't you use your own money? He would have had two gifts then.'

'Because you didn't give me time,' Nick said, and answered the monk's grave nod of acknowledgement with a similar courtesy, and drew Judi on.

'I wanted to give him a gift myself,' she fumed.

'And you have. And no doubt gained merit in the process.' There was no flippancy in Nick's tone, only a deep respect for another philosophy, as he went on,

'It isn't done for a woman to give directly to a monk. If you had waited for a moment, he would have spread out a cloth for you to place your offering on, and then he would have taken it up from there.'

He looked down into her indignant face. 'That's the way things are, here. Be thankful that I prevented you from committing a social gaffe. As Pet said, these things are difficult for a person from another culture to understand, but when in Rome...'

Pet had not said 'another culture'. She had said 'an outsider', and the mention of her name blew a cool draught across the ease between them. Nick watched doubt and uncertainty chase away the indignation, and consoled her.

'Don't let it worry you. Tolerance is Thailand's middle name. If you had given your offering to the monk yourself, he would have accepted your kindness, and forgiven your ignorance. But it's better not to offend if you can possibly help it.'

'How am I to know?'

'I'll guide you,' Nick promised airily, and did just that by taking her arm and steering her on to a water bus that drew up at the side of the canal.

'This will take us to the floating market,' he explained. 'It's had to move some distance away since the canals were filled in in the centre of the city.'

So much for Judi's relief at not having to take a taxi! But the slatted wooden seats provided more room, and the awning-topped boat was not as confined as a taxi, and carried other passengers besides, and although Nick put his arm across the back of the seat behind her he made no attempt actually to drape it across her shoulders in public.

Was this another taboo? Judi wondered, and learned much later that it was. For the moment, she was grateful for the distancing, and forgot the small contretemps as the water bus cruised past stilt houses raised on their piles above the muddy canal waters, providing perfect diving-boards for children who made gleeful use of the natural swimming pool above which they lived, showing off as children will the world over when they know they have an interested audience.

Judi was so absorbed in watching them that it came as a surprise when Nick rose to his feet and said, 'This is as far as we go.'

Remembering the ardour of his kisses the evening before, she felt tempted to ask if that applied to their relationship as well, but she did not quite dare, and grasped at the diversion offered by a packed array of boats that served as floating market stalls to check her unruly thoughts.

With their craft crammed high with a colourful array of merchandise of every description, the basket-hatted boaters poled frantically, jostling with each other for the best vantage-points against the wooden walkways fixed on either side of the canal, and now ahustle with the new influx of customers brought in by the water bus.

Tourists were few in number, Judi noticed; the heat was still too intense for most Western tastes, but for the moment anyway she was able to forget it in the fascination of this novel method of doing the weekly shopping. She attached herself tightly to Nick's side, unwilling to miss a minute of the teeming, multi-coloured scene, which he paused now and then to photograph, and dictate to her a brief caption to go with the shot.

'Durian fruit . . . d-u-r . . . what's the matter?' He paused as Judi forgot her pen, grabbed for her handkerchief, and flattened it over her mouth and nose.

'Ugh! What an awful smell!'

A foetid reek rose from a boatload of the green, spiky-looking fruit which Nick was describing. To Judi they resembled nothing so much as green hedgehogs, and she gagged and complained, 'That boater ought to be run out of business. The fruit's going rotten.'

'It's nothing of the kind,' Nick contradicted, and to her disgust he leaned down and bargained with the owner for one of the offending fruit, and held it out to show to her.

She backed away hastily. 'Give it back,' she begged. 'It smells awful.'

'The smell might be awful, but the taste is great.'

Nick delved into his pocket and fished out a useful-looking penknife. He fingered open one of the blades, and used it to cut through the hard green outer layer, while dextrously managing to evade the cruel-looking spikes. He held out a piece towards her.

'Try it.'

Judi rebelled. 'You can't trick me into eating that, like you did the curry.'

'I told you, I don't play childish tricks. You ordered the curry yourself.'

She had not ordered the way Nick played tricks with her heart. She blamed its antics now on the smell, shook her head stubbornly, and Nick said, 'You're missing out on a treat. They're considered a great delicacy by the locals. They're about the most expensive of all the fruits you can buy out here, which should tell you something.'

What the fruit was telling Judi was outrageous. She dared not allow herself to imagine what it tasted like. The formidable odour assaulted her nostrils with the same force that Nick's charisma assaulted her senses, and tormented by both she flashed, 'I don't believe you. If it's such a delicacy, why didn't I see any on the plane, or at the hotel?'

'Because of the smell, of course. It ranks with garlic for pong, and you enjoyed a garlic-flavoured dish in the restaurant last night.'

He was altogether too aware. Judi shot back, 'Rank is the operative word.'

'Have it your own way.' Nick shrugged. He cut a piece of the fruit for himself, put it in his mouth and chewed appreciatively. 'Mmm. Lovely. It's a good thirst-quencher, too.'

He was sadistic. Without having realised it before, Judi suddenly discovered that her throat and mouth were parched. The heat had increased without her noticing, but now it made its force felt. It beat back at her from the wooden walkway, shimmered from the patches of water visible between the jockeying boats, and taunted her with the lack of anything drinkable until Nick chose to take a break and head for whatever restaurant offered itself; and, now his own thirst was quenched, that might not be for ages.

There appeared to be no restaurant in the immediate vicinity. She faced Nick once more, to find his hand held out, still offering her the piece of fruit to try.

The portion reeked, and her pride as well as her nose revolted against accepting it, but Nick's amused look challenged her, and her throat cried out for moisture.

'Suspend belief,' he urged her. 'Hold your nose and eat it.'

He pressed the fruit into her hand, minus its spikes, she noticed, glancing down at the scars on the rind that told her Nick had first cut them off, so that they would not stick in and hurt her fingers.

The small consideration sent a curious feeling shafting through Judi, but she ignored it and opened her mouth to beg, 'Take it away, I won't touch it,' and found only a croak coming from her arid throat.

In vain she touched her parched lips with her tongue, but it had no moisture to offer, and tormented beyond endurance she did as he told her to, and stuffed her handkerchief over her nose, and bit into the fruit.

The luscious flesh yielded to her small teeth; it was creamy and moist, and unbelievably delicious. Incredulity widened her eyes, and Nick said, 'Now you know why the locals enjoy them so much. Have another piece.'

It was nectar in her parched mouth. Judi swallowed her pride and accepted the second piece, and her tongue and throat were able to return to their duties, refreshed enough to threaten, 'If you say I told you so, I'll push you into the canal.'

'Try,' Nick suggested softly, and their glances met and crossed, like drawn swords. Judi knew that if she thrust first Nick would have no compunction in thrusting back, and his blade would be a lot sharper than her own.

Hastily she shifted ground, and mumbled, 'Another time,' and fished out a moistened cleansing pad from her shoulder-bag, and busied herself ridding her hands and face of traces of fruit juice.

When she recovered enough courage to look back at Nick, he said, 'If you've finished your cat-lick, we'll walk on to the street market. It isn't far away, and we can get some lunch there at a Chinese restaurant I know. I've got all the shots I need from here.'

'I've finished,' Judi assented, and breathed more freely when they took to the streets again, and left the canal behind them. Nick walked in silence, for so long that Judi was driven to banality to break it.

'After watching you take all those shots, I shall have to have one of the firm's brochures as a souvenir,' she said tritely, and drew an oblique glance from Nick.

'The work we're doing now is for next year's brochures. They won't be out until the spring.'

Sudden depression descended upon Judi, mocked by the bright sunshine. Where would they all be by then? What would they be doing? And with whom?

Nick cut across her conjectures with, 'As souvenirs go, a holiday brochure seems a modest ambition. Isn't there something else you'd like to take home with you?'

It was on the tip of Judi's tongue to retort, 'You,' and she slapped the mischievous urge into submission, shocked as she wondered what had prompted it.

The contents of a nearby stall suggested a ready answer, and she blurted, 'I'd love one of those dolls dressed as classical dancers, like those we saw yesterday.'

The street market opened out round them, more sedate than the floating market, in that the traders each had their own unassailable positions, and relied on crying their wares to attract custom.

The result was deafening but effective, and turned her to a stall selling dolls, in competition with the one next to it. Judi did not particularly want a doll, but it served to distract her unwelcome thoughts, and she could always give it to Louise's small niece when she returned home.

Nick said, 'Those dolls are ten a penny. If you want one that will keep its value, buy a Piya doll. They're craftsman made, although of course they're more expensive.'

Judi sent him a surprised look. Had Nick got the same outlook as Robert, seeing everything in terms of money? It went against the little she knew of him. He had struck her as being a person who did not care a jot for the monetary value of anything, except perhaps for his working equipment, but her instincts could be wrong.

She answered him stubbornly, 'I want one of these,' and exchanged coins for the doll with a defensive, 'It's got a friendly face,' without bothering to haggle over the cost.

Nick criticised, 'You've been conned.'

A closer inspection of her tawdry purchase justified his remark, but it served to harden Judi's defence of her action, and she flashed, 'I've paid the right price, if it's worth it to me, whatever you might think. We don't all view everything in terms of money.'

'Quite right, too,' Nick agreed aggravatingly, and left Judi unsure whether she had misjudged him or not, but he left her with no time to ponder. He teased, 'Do you need a friendly face so badly, Judi, that you have to buy a doll?'

Her head jerked up, but curiously there was no teasing in his expression, only a narrow-eyed probing that made her slide up her defences against him, and respond stiffly, 'I've got loads of friends back home. I want the doll for the niece of one of them.'

'Make sure it's safe before you give it to a child,' Nick cautioned. 'Sometimes there are loose pins and things in these tourist trifles, that aren't so securely fastened as they might be.'

What a curious mixture the man was. He seemed to be as hard as iron one moment, driving her to hate him for it, and the next he showed an unexpectedly caring side to his nature which disarmed her defences, and laid her open to...

Judi braked hard on her thoughts, and Nick slid into the void with a deceptively gentle, 'Where is home to you?'

Caught off guard, Judi replied, 'London. Or at least, we live just outside London, on the borders of Surrey.'

'Stockbroker country,' Nick gibed, and Judi's lips tightened, and felt strangely reluctant to answer when he pressed, 'Who is "we"?'

'My parents and me. Did you think I meant a boyfriend?'

His question was an affront, and her tone resented it, and resented even more that he should think he had a right to probe into her background. It was nothing whatever to do with him. There was not the slightest reason why she should not tell him, but there were all sorts of reasons why she suddenly did not want to, although if she had been pressed to explain, she could not have named one of them.

She headed off any further questions by throwing his own back at him. 'Where is home to you?' and he answered her readily enough.

'Shropshire. It's the family home, really. My aunt and uncle live in it now, but it's a great, rambling barn of a place, and I use the one wing of it for myself. That way, we can lead completely separate lives without getting under each other's feet.'

It sounded as if it might be a farm, or perhaps a vicarage, Judi thought vaguely, and tried another question.

'You must spend quite a lot of time away from home. Dave says you're an authority on the Far East. And you were in London when we first bumped into one another.'

'When you bumped into me, you mean.'

He did not give an inch, and he intercepted her glare with a cool look that accepted his own lack of blame, and raised Judi's hackles, but before she could think up a retort he went on, 'I keep a flat in London, near to Marble Arch. I do a lot of commissioned work, as well as writing and lecturing. The flat serves as an office and a work-place, and saves me the bother of constantly booking hotel rooms when I have to come up to town.'

A flat near to Marble Arch coincided with Nick's choice of car, Judi thought. Both hideously expensive. She asked curiously, 'Would you like to live permanently out East?'

'No. I love it out here, but my roots are in Shropshire, and I wouldn't live anywhere else on a permanent basis. My flat is just a convenient bolt-hole. It isn't home.'

That was another aspect of Nick which she had not suspected. A deeper, home-loving side to his nature that needed to return to his roots. When she returned to hers, Judi reflected, she too would need a bolt-hole in which to shelter from the storm that would surely break about her head when she gave Robert back his ring. She thrust the problem into the future and said, 'Louise, my friend who runs the language school, is on a walking-holiday through Shropshire, with her husband. She asked me to go with her.'

'Do you wish you had?'

It would have been nice if he had said, 'I'm glad you didn't,' and the omission left a small bleakness that Judi covered with anger. Nick was so sure of himself. So self-contained. If she had gone with Louise she would not have met him, and she did not know whether to be glad or sorry at the fall of the dice, so she evaded his question with, 'I had to escort the children back here.'

'Do you know the border country back home?'

'No. I've never been there, although I've often thought I'd like to, some day.'

'That day will come when we leave here.'

Judi's head jerked up, startled. 'I shan't be coming with you to Shropshire.'

His look held sudden steel. 'You agreed to see this job through to completion.'

'I know. But I assumed it would finish when you left Thailand. You said it would mean two or three weeks here. You didn't say anything about the work continuing when we got back to England.'

'All our time in this country is spent in actually collecting the brochure material. The nitty gritty of sorting and collating the photographs and the captions has to be done somewhere less expensive. The travel firm doesn't pay astronomical hotel bills for any longer than is absolutely necessary.'

Judi's brows knitted. The possibility of continuing with Nick afterwards had not occurred to her. It was disturbing. Exciting. Her pulses responded, and she tried to still their wild throbbing with, 'I shall be needed back at the language school when I return home.'

That was an untruth. The school would be closed for several weeks, but her independent spirit rebelled at Nick's arrogant assumption that he had the right to dictate her movements for an indefinite period.

'Schools don't reassemble until the autumn term. That still gives you a few weeks, which will be time enough to finish what you started.'

Her erratic pulse-beat questioned exactly what she had started, and made Judi persist stubbornly, 'I've got something else planned.'

'Have you booked a holiday?'

Judi knew that he must read the answer on her face. She did not lie easily, and it showed, and Nick's abrupt, 'Well?' dragged a reluctant, 'No,' from her lips, that she scorned herself for giving.

If this was strong, self-assured womanhood, it did not seem to be working. She should have asserted herself, told him to get someone else when he returned to England. She did try.

'You can easily get another secretary.'

'Who won't know which caption applies to what photograph. You appear on most of the shots yourself, so you won't need me to explain the link. I need to be able to leave you to do the job yourself, if necessary, while I get on with other things.'

He did not explain what he meant by other things, and Judi was too indignant to ask. She rasped, 'Surely you don't need to drag me all the way to Shropshire for that? What about your flat in London? I could travel up to town daily, the same as I do to the school.'

'The flat is being re-decorated.'

He had got an answer for everything, and used work to prevent Judi from finding out any more excuses for herself. He seemed to want a photograph of almost every stall they came to, and dictated at a furious pace as he worked, twice the amount of information he had used on any previous captions.

His voice drove on and on, never slackening speed, and facts and figures, and odd snippets of history, came hurtling towards Judi like components on some remorseless conveyor-belt. If he continued like this, it would take more than a few weeks to collate all the information he was gathering when they returned to England.

The heat intensified, and Judi's hands grew sticky with perspiration and acted as a brake on her speed, until at last she was driven to beg, 'Wait a minute, do, while I wipe my hands dry. They're sticking to the paper, and holding me up.'

Nick seemed to be indefatigable, but her own immunity to the heat was not so great as she had tried to make him believe, and she wriggled under the discomfort of clothes sticking to her body, and hair clinging in limp strands to her damp forehead, getting in her way as she bent her head over her notebook.

A swarm of flies hovered over her head, waiting their chance to dive in and settle on her face, and sip at the salty moisture that ran down her cheeks, making her feel as if her very lifeblood was being drawn out of her by the merciless sun.

It was humiliating to melt in front of Nick. In spite of patches of dampness darkening his own shirt, he showed no obvious signs of distress, and the contrast of his calm immunity made Judi swat the harder at the flies, and mutter crossly, 'I wish I'd got one of those magic ray guns, to shoot at these beastly pests.'

'Try this instead.'

His look mocked her discomfort, but he turned aside to a nearby stall and exchanged coins for a purchase, flipped it open with deft fingers, and handed the painted paper fan to Judi with the remark, 'This is much more feminine than a ray gun.'

The fan was large and bright, and painted with gaudy butterflies, and as Judi waved it gratefully in front of her face, the draught of blissfully cool air wafting across her hot cheeks was tinged with the aromatic sandalwood used for the delicate wooden struts. It brought her instant relief and sent the flies off to seek other victims, and she breathed a heartfelt, 'Bless you for this. You can carry on now.'

'Is that a go-ahead to work, or an invitation to play?'

His smile teased, and for a wild moment Judi wondered what he would do if she said, 'Play,' and wondered aghast, what on earth has come over me? I must have a touch of the sun.

She fanned frantically to cool her scarlet cheeks, but Nick's soft taunt reached behind the fan and through to her skin, to prick on nerves already too rawly aware of him.

'You can't hide behind your fan from me, Judi.'

'Who said I was trying to? I thought you were going this way.' Judi turned away, pretending to look along another alley between the market stalls. 'We haven't been on that side of the market yet.'

'I did. And we're not going to that side of the market. It smells.'

'I can cope with durian fruit, now I know what it is.'

'That's the area for meat, not fruit, and the smells are much fiercer. They come from dried fish, and unmentionable parts of pig, and there are literally millions of flies. Come this way instead.'

Nick's way took them among exotic flowers, which young girls with faces that matched their merchandise wove into garlands.

Judi gasped her pleasure, and quivered as Nick said, 'Some of the garlands are meant for the shrines. But not all.' He did not say what they were for, and suddenly Judi could not ask, when he bought one and dropped it round her shoulders.

'That's another souvenir,' he told her gravely. 'It will help to erase the memory of the smells.'

'I love it all, even the smells,' Judi declared stoutly, and knew that she spoke the truth. They were all part of the magic tapestry. But which was the canvas? The market, or Nick?

She jinked away from answering her own question, and said, 'I've never been in an Eastern market before.'

'Not even while you were in India?' His surprise was evident.

Judi shook her head. She had not visited the markets with Robert, and the behaviour of her pulse questioned her wisdom in visiting them now with Nick.

The perfume from her garland rose in a heady incense to tease her nostrils. It mingled with the sharp scent of sandalwood from her fan, and the penetrating smoke of burning joss-sticks from a nearby stall. The sharp scent of citrus fruit vied with dried spices, all adding to an intoxicating mixture that made Judi's head spin.

She swayed slightly on her feet, and a vendor selling dried chicken pieces speared on bamboo sticks gave her an excuse for her unsteadiness as being caused by hunger. As if reading her thoughts, Nick glanced at his watch.

'It's time we ate, but not from his basket. Do you like Chinese?'

'I'm so empty, I'm willing to try anything.'

'Even eating with chopsticks?'

Nick wielded them with expert dexterity, but to Judi they were a new experience, and her amateur attempts to capture pieces of the tempting stir-fry left more on her plate than in her mouth.

Nick was a new experience, and one not so easily resolved as when the smiling proprietor of the restaurant proffered a knife and fork instead, and at Nick's request wrapped up the chopsticks as another souvenir for Judi to practise on later when she felt less hungry.

Would longer contact with Nick increase her appetite for his company, after they returned to England? she wondered uneasily, and pretended an interest in her food which she no longer felt, to evade the question.

The proprietor greeted Nick as an old friend, and seated them in the window at what he described as, 'Your usual table, Professor,' so that they could watch the street scene outside while they ate. With the help of the more familiar cutlery, Judi was able to cope with her meal while her eyes feasted on the colour and movement of the market outside.

They talked easily while they ate. Judi commented, 'It will have to be a huge brochure, to fit in all the potted histories. I must have taken down dozens this morning.'

Nick replied idly, 'They weren't all for the brochure. I'm writing a book on the country as well. A lot of the stuff we are collecting will go into that.'

His 'we' gave her a warm feeling. A book was more personal, and more lasting, than a tourist brochure, and it felt good to know that she would be part of it.

He added, 'That photograph of Dave and Pet, wading across the flood, for instance. That will go into the book, and not the brochure, for obvious reasons.'

His casual words brought back the feel of his arms round her, carrying her across the flood, and churned the warmth inside her into a simmering cauldron. As if to echo the disturbance, another one flared in the street outside the window.

A furious screeching drew an instant crowd of onlookers, and a commotion broke out in front of the nearest stall. Nick surmised shrewdly, 'A thief,' and seconds later the boiling centre of the crowd spilled through, and a youth fled, confirming his guess.

Several people started to pursue him, but the heat soon evaporated their anger, and people resumed the serious business of bargaining as if nothing had happened.

Judi said, 'It's just the same, even here,' and a cloud shadowed her face.

Nick answered gently, *'Mai pen rai,'* and meeting Judi's puzzled look he explained, 'It's Thai for "never mind". Accept what you can't help. Human nature is the same the world over.'

'Human nature should know better than to treat other people so shabbily. It turns civilisation into a lie.'

A bitterness she could not quite control sharpened Judi's voice, and Nick's eyes narrowed, keen on her face.

'You accept human frailty yourself. If you don't, why is it that you don't wear any jewellery on your travels, except for a cheap watch?'

For that very reason, but Nick's eyes, Judi noticed with a sense of shock, rested not on her neck, which might otherwise be adorned by a chain, or her wrist, minus a bracelet, but on the third, ringless finger of her left hand.

Which was in itself a living lie, since she would not be morally free until she had returned Robert's ring.

CHAPTER FIVE

JUDI's garland was already beginning to wilt by the time they returned to the hotel. She regarded it sadly. Perhaps if she put it in water, it might perk up again, she hoped.

She wanted to keep the garland forever, along with the doll and the chopsticks, but Nick shook his head.

'You're wasting your time. Flowers in the tropics only last for a day.'

Here today, and gone tomorrow. Was that how Nick viewed love? The thought tracked unheralded across her mind, and brought back her depression as she made her way to her room to freshen up before starting to type her morning notes.

Pet came along the corridor a second too soon to enable Judi to escape through her room door. The older women eyed her handful of souvenirs and sneered, 'Tourist trash.'

Her look included Judi herself in the description, and she fumed inwardly as Pet continued, before she could retort, 'Those garlands are meant to be given to you by someone else. You don't buy them for yourself.'

'I didn't,' Judi snapped, and, leaving Pet standing open-mouthed in the corridor, she stalked through her room door and slammed it behind her, and thought unrepentantly, let her make what she likes of that, while she wondered what meaning there was to the particular garland which Nick had placed around her neck.

The question teased her mind while she was typing up her notes, but perforce had to remain unvoiced when Nick came in to collect them later, and then returned to his room to continue with his own work. He appeared briefly at dinner, but went back to his room immediately afterwards to sort out the equipment he needed to take with him on the coming trip to Chiang Mai.

Judi grabbed the opportunity to chat up Dave, to Pet's evident chagrin. The older woman was used to being 'one of the boys' on the team, and did not relish being usurped, Judi guessed shrewdly, and redoubled her efforts. It was only when Dave himself began to show signs of restlessness that she desisted.

'I think I'll go upstairs and pack,' she said, and with a lingering smile at Dave, and a nod in Pet's direction, she bade them both goodnight, and thought with satisfaction as she made her way up to her room, that was a good start. I'll have another try tomorrow.

Her behaviour left Pet in a quandary when they all met at the minibus, parked in front of the hotel the following morning. Each of them carried only a small bag containing the basic necessities to see them through a few days away from the hotel. Nick had the most luggage, because of his photographic equipment, and he bade them briskly, 'Sling your gear in the back and jump in. I'll drive to start with. The rest of you can spread yourselves. There's plenty of room.'

Judi watched Pet interestedly to see if her strategy had worked sufficiently to make the older woman want to sit beside Dave, in a dog-in-the-manger attempt to claim him as well. Or would she try for the seat beside Nick?

Pet hesitated, and then plumped for the seat beside Nick. If only Pet knew, she is playing right into my hands, Judi thought gleefully. She did not want to sit beside Nick herself. His sharp glance took in the fact that she was carrying the fan which he'd given her the day before, and he commented, 'The air is fresher in the mountains. You'll feel more comfortable at Chiang Mai.'

She would never feel comfortable anywhere within range of Nick, and Judi's reaction on awakening and seeing the souvenirs of their trip round the markets warned her that the further she could remove herself from him, the better.

The moment her eyes were open, she found herself instinctively feeling round for the chopsticks, with the eagerness of a child reaching out to see if birthday presents were still there. Only her feelings were not those of a child, and uneasily she thrust the chopsticks into the bottom of her suitcase, out of sight, and escaped to the shower, where she found the garland, with its flowers faded, as Nick had said they would, floating like a sad wreath in the water of her washbasin.

With hands that were suddenly unsteady she rescued it, and mourned the fact that it could not speak, and tell her for what purpose it had been woven. And purchased. The odd behaviour of her pulse said that it might be better if she remained in ignorance, and before she could follow her train of thought any further she broke off one small bloom that was not so badly faded as the others and tucked it in with the chopsticks, thrusting the rest into the waste-bin with the comforting knowledge that they would be removed before her return.

Judi ignored the array of empty seats in the minibus, snuggled up beside Dave, pretending not to notice his look of surprise.

'This is cosier than sitting on our own,' she smiled, encouraged by Pet's glare from in front.

The countryside began to change as they left the city and its traffic behind, and the road rose gradually into the foothills of the distant mountains, leaving behind the sticky humidity of the plains.

It was still hot, but as Nick had promised the air became fresher, more so with each mile as the road took them higher into the hills. Judi breathed deeply, relishing its sweetness, and returned to her campaign with renewed vigour.

The passing scenery gave her the perfect excuse to ply Dave with questions, to which he replied patiently enough, although disappointingly he did not possess Nick's extensive knowledge, nor his sensitive ability to extract from it those odd bits of human interest which made their photographic forays together such an unforgettable experience.

Nick himself made no attempt to take part in the conversation. His attention was concentrated on surviving, first the city traffic, and then the deteriorating road conditions as they headed far out into the countryside; and Judi blamed the peculiar rigidity of his neck and shoulders as they appeared above the top of the driving seat on tension caused by the hazardous road conditions.

Pet spoke to him once or twice, but she received only monosyllabic replies, and eventually she relapsed into a sulky silence, with ample time to reflect upon her mistake in allowing Judi to sit beside Dave and monopolise his attention.

They paused briefly to stretch their legs and eat the packed lunch provided by the hotel, before they pressed on. As the hours passed, weariness stemmed the flow of Judi's questions.

A comfort stop later, Dave took a turn at the wheel, and Judi's languor temporarily vanished under a racing pulse as she waited with bated breath for Nick to choose his seat in the back of the bus.

Would he come to sit beside her, in Dave's place?

She could feel tension oozing from Pet, telling her that the older woman was on the same wavelength, and Judi felt her silent triumph when Nick answered their unspoken question by calmly taking the window-seat directly opposite to herself, and spreading himself across it, so that it was impossible for anyone else to attempt to share it with him.

Was it a deliberate snub, making sure that she would not slip across the aisle to join him? Pique and dis-appointment warred inside Judi, and she despised herself for both. She did not want to sit beside Nick. But without Dave's bulk as a buffer, her own seat was much too large for her petite frame, and when the minibus restarted she found herself being jolted round like a pea in a pod, not least because Dave was not so adept at missing the numerous pot-holes which pockmarked the road at every yard.

In desperation, Judi copied Nick and jammed herself into the seat corner, with her back to the window, a move that brought herself and Nick facing one another across the aisle.

With a curious thrill, she saw that Nick was already asleep, catnapping with the easy ability of the seasoned traveller to conserve his energy for when he might need to draw upon it later.

Dave had his eyes firmly fixed on the road ahead, and Pet was now too busy watching for pot-holes herself, and bracing her bulk in her seat to meet them, to be able to turn round; safe from observation herself, Judi was able to study Nick at her leisure.

His sleeping face looked curiously vulnerable. Her breath developed a peculiar catchy quality as her eyes rested on his relaxed features. The strength still showed, but sleep erased the sternness, and stripped ten years from his age, and the bright laughter-lines about his eyes and lips, which said he laughed a lot when he was with friends, were more evident now that he was no longer conscious to control them.

In spite of stuffing his equipment bag behind him for a pillow, his head rolled with the movement of the bus, and Judi felt an awful longing to curl her arm about it and hold it still, cradling it against her shoulder so that she could stroke back the crisp, tawny waves that had fallen in coloured strands across his high forehead.

Such was the intensity of her longing that her fingers flexed involuntarily, feeling the rich crispness of his hair stroke through her fingers.

She might as well risk tangling them in a lion's mane; and, if she tried, this lion would surely wake up and bite. Her finger-ends actually hurt at the prospect, and unconsciously she drew them close together on her lap, and nursed them to her, as if trying to nurse away the wound, and forced herself to study Nick's features instead.

Relaxed in sleep, his jaw had fallen slightly, and parted his lips, and his teeth gleamed in a shaft of

sunlight shining through the bus window. The cleft
in his chin was not so evident from where Judi sat.
To see it properly, she needed to have her head resting
against his shoulder, just above the region of his heart.

Needed to?

Her mind posed the question, and her heart responded with a wild thudding that actually hurt, so
much that it drew a gasp from her lips, and another
when her eyes rose from his chin and discovered that
his were wide open and watching her.

'What's the verdict?' he drawled.

Judi went rigid. She felt her cheeks go scarlet, and
then white. Hurriedly she swung her legs from the
seat, and turned her face towards the front of the bus,
so that it presented a less revealing profile to Nick's
probing gaze, and mumbled, 'I ... you ...'

A pot-hole saved her. At that moment the bus
wheels were engulfed in a particularly ferocious
example, and the resulting jolt clicked Judi's teeth
together. Fortunately, her tongue was not between
them, otherwise she would have been rendered in-
capable of answering him, but it gave her a split second's grace in which to recover, and the perfect answer
to shoot back at him, 'Guilty. These pot-holes are the
absolute limit They're enough to break every bone
in your body.'

She felt quite proud of the way in which she had
ducked Nick's salvo, and then she met the glint in his
eyes, and it told her that the reckoning was not can-
celled, but only postponed.

Soon afterwards, they reached Chiang Mai, and
Dave stopped at a hotel that looked about the equiv-
alent of their accommodation in Bangkok. With relief
Judi reached for her bag.

Nick checked her. 'This is the tourist hotel. We're not staying here ourselves, only having dinner. Our own accommodation is more basic on this trip, and further into the hills. That way we shan't have to waste time trekking back here each night.'

Trekking was a good description, Judi thought ruefully when they resumed their journey, and she wondered uneasily what Nick had meant when he described their accommodation as basic.

The road degenerated into little more than a jungle track. Thick forest rose on either side of them, and if she had not been so travel-weary Judi would have gloried in the wealth of birdlife which she glimpsed flitting and calling among the trees.

But all her weary body longed for at the moment was a long wallow in a hot bath, to ease her aching frame, and the comfort of a soft bed afterwards. The bamboo huts circling a wide clearing among the trees did not look as if they would offer either, and a horrid premonition seized Judi as Dave stopped the minibus in front of one of them, turned to Nick, and said, 'I booked one big bungalow for all of us. That way, it gives you the living-room as a work-room, and the bedrooms are big enough to share, without us getting under one another's feet too much.'

She and Pet would get under one another's feet in an empty exhibition hall, Judi thought, and knew an impish desire to suggest a mix 'n' match arrangement instead, and wondered, if she did, which mix would best match. Nick cut across such rebel thoughts with a brisk, 'Make yourselves at home. You two girls choose which room you want, and Dave and I will camp in the other.'

'Camp' was hardly a fair description, Judi discovered with relief when she followed Pet into the nearest bedroom. The older woman tossed her case on to the bed nearer to the window, and threw at Judi, 'I'll take this one,' with a challenging look, and no 'do you mind?' or any offer to allow her companion the first choice.

It was Pet's second mistake of the day. The other bed was tucked away in a corner, far removed from the light, but it was much nearer to the shower cubicle, and Judi took immediate advantage of the fact.

She returned a short time later feeling completely refreshed, to find Pet slumped on her bed, tiredness evident in every wilting line of her frame. Quick compassion seized Judi. She could never like Pet, but her naturally warm heart could not help feeling sympathy for the older woman's plight.

When Pet had been in her twenties, trekking about the world arranging exotic tours for other people must have seemed a glamorous job, but now, in her late and much less energetic thirties, and having done the same thing endlessly every year for nearly a couple of decades, the work must have lost its former attraction, and from the look of Pet now she was finding the tinsel distinctly tarnished.

Judi forced a conciliatory note into her voice, and enquired, 'Are you very tired? It's been a long day. The water's lovely and warm, if you want a shower.'

'I'm *never* tired when I'm travelling,' Pet snapped back, and turned on Judi furiously. 'But I am sick and tired of listening to you, trying to make up to Dave. Have you got no sense? He's almost old enough to be your father.'

'Do you think that age matters?' Judi asked inno-
cently, and sent a speculative glance out of the
window.

The swift tropical darkness had fallen while she was
showering, but the lights from the cabin were sufficient to make the object of their conversation clearly
visible as he manoeuvred the minibus to a more convenient parking slot out of the way.

Judi said slyly, 'You don't seem to think that age
matters with Nick.'

'How dare you?'

'Why be coy? You like Nick, don't you?'

How would she answer the same question, if it were
applied to herself? Judi wondered, and jinked away
from the answer. She hurried on, 'I think Dave's nice.
In fact, he's quite a poppet.'

If she was able to force Pet to confront her own,
even less suitable attraction to Nick, it might bring
her to her senses, Judi reflected, and wondered if her
own motives were entirely altruistic.

She comforted herself with the thought that if she
could help Dave to attain his heart's desire it might
also solve Pet's problem for her as well. Pet could not
go on forever tramping around the globe, and a nice
little cottage somewhere in England, with Dave for
company, would provide the ideal solution.

Feeling rather like a universal Miss Fix-it, she persisted, 'I'm going out to join Dave now, while you
have your shower,' and escaped from the room before
Pet could answer her.

Judi met Dave coming up the steps of the small
veranda attached to the cabin. He, too, looked weary,
as if he wanted a shower and a rest, but the veranda

was within clear sight of the bedroom windows, and the opportunity was too good to miss.

She gave him a beaming smile and, leaning over the veranda rail, she pointed vaguely in the direction of the other cabins and asked brightly, 'What's that?'

'What's what?' Unable to see what she was pointing at, perforce Dave had to come to stand beside her.

'I thought I saw something move, in the shadow of that cabin over there.'

'Maybe it was a small animal, looking for scraps. The forest comes alive at night.'

'How very wise of it,' Judi murmured provocatively, and pivoted to face him. 'The romance of the East,' she simpered. 'Can't you feel it, Dave?'

What Dave felt was obvious embarrassment, and Judi had to resist an urge to giggle as she slid her arms slowly up his crumpled shirt-front, and stood on tiptoe to link them round his neck.

It was a long stretch for her much shorter height, but somehow she made herself elastic, and hung on, hoping the effect would look good from where she guessed Pet must be watching them from behind the bedroom blinds.

Dave raised his hands and caught at Judi's arms, growling, 'Judi, don't. I'm nearly old enough to be your father.' He tried ineffectually to turn his embarrassment into a joke. 'I'm the wrong star sign for you. We'd fight.'

'What about Pet's star sign?'

'We match. But why this sudden interest in astrology? I thought you didn't believe in it.'

'I don't. But if you want to get anywhere with Pet, you'd better start trying to convince her that it works.'

Dave said stiffly, 'Leave Pet out of it.'

'Gladly. But you can't, if my guess is right. You are in love with her, aren't you?'

Poor man! Judi thought. He's not liking this one little bit. Underneath that hard-bitten exterior, Dave was actually shy.

'So?'

Judi gave him a little shake. 'Can't you see, I'm trying to make Pet jealous, you goose?' she whispered. 'It's my guess she's watching us now, from the bedroom window, and if she sees me making headway with you, she'll want to compete.'

'Feline!'

'Not at all. It's human nature.'

Not her own, Judi contradicted silently. After Robert, she considered no man worth competing for. Her mind disposed of Robert, and returned to more immediate problems. She urged, 'Go in and convince her. I'll help you to lay the foundations, but it's up to you to do the building.'

Dave frowned. 'Are you sure it's Pet you're trying to make jealous?'

'Who else?'

'Nick?' he suggested.

'*Nick?* You must be joking.' Judi's laugh exploded from her lips, and sounded curiously high-pitched. 'Whatever you say about our star signs, Nick's not my type. I've got no liking for lions, and absolutely no wish to be eaten by this one. So far as Nick is concerned, you can forget him.'

'That's all right, then.'

Was it? Judi wondered uneasily, but Dave's next question gave her no time to answer her own.

'How did you guess, about the way I feel for Pet?'

'I didn't need the stars to tell me,' Judi twinkled. 'It's obvious to anyone with eyes to see.'

'I still don't see why you...'

'I owe you something for getting me this job, that's why.' There was no need for her to overdo it, she reflected, and confess to Dave that she was also using him as an antidote to Nick.

'You little minx!' A moment of incredulity later, and Judi felt laughter rumble through Dave. 'But I love you for it.' With a deep-throated chuckle, he swept her into his arms and kissed her soundly. 'There. Do you think that will look realistic enough from the window?'

'Try kissing Pet instead.' Judi drew back, pink-cheeked. 'It might work.'

'If it doesn't, it won't be for the want of trying.'

'Don't let on to anybody that this is only pretend between you and me,' Judi cautioned him, 'or all my work will have been wasted.'

'I'll guard the secret with my life, even from Nick,' Dave promised, and teased, 'I hope you haven't found the work too much of a chore.'

'I've loved every minute of it,' Judi assured him solemnly, and, stretching up again, she planted a kiss on the tip of his chin for good measure. 'Now go ahead, and good luck, and if Pet wants another push in the right direction, don't forget, I'm ready... and willing,' she added wickedly.

'It's a pity you're not just as willing to get on with the job I'm paying you for,' Nick's voice snarled from just behind her. Hot with embarrassment herself now, Judi spun round to face the furious glitter of two tawny eyes.

She had not heard him approach. His cat-like tread had brought him to within touching distance without her noticing a thing, and Judi wondered raggedly how much he had seen and heard. She cringed from the prospect of Nick putting the same construction on her flippant, 'and willing', that Dave himself had done in the hotel foyer when they had first met.

Nick snapped, 'In case it's escaped your notice, the typewriter is on the table in the cabin, already plugged in, and I want the stack of papers I've put beside it to be typed up before tomorrow morning.'

Dave protested, 'Surely it's a bit late to start work tonight, Nick? We've been travelling all day, and Judi must be just as tired as the rest of us.'

'I warned her that it wouldn't be easy, when she took on the job. She said then that she wouldn't wilt.'

'And I won't,' Judi snapped, before Dave could come to her defence again.

Nick had not warned her that he could be cruel, sadistic, and a complete male chauvinist. 'I'll finish every word before I go to bed,' she choked, and bit her tongue to prevent, 'if it kills me', from coming out.

'Good,' Nick applauded derisively. 'That should make you want nothing more than to go to sleep the moment your head hits the pillow.'

How dared he? Judi longed to hit Nick as she stalked past him, pausing only to throw back at Dave a taut, 'Forget it, Dave. Remember what we agreed,' when the older man began to argue,

'I say, Nick, that's a bit below the belt. Judi had a reason . . .'

Her eyes widened as she confronted the stack of hand-written notes tossed down beside the typewriter, uncharacteristically haphazard. Nick usually handed the work to her neatly clipped together, but now it was strewn across the table, and two of the papers had drifted on to the floor as if he had flung them down in passing, uncaring of how or where they landed.

Judi bent to pick up the two sheets, and froze as a pair of familiar sandals came into her line of vision through the door. They halted at the entrance to the room, and exerting an immense effort of self-control she made herself reach out unhurriedly for the second piece of paper, with an arm that felt suddenly nerveless.

Her fingers scrabbled twice at its smooth surface before she was able to get enough grip to lift it and bring it to join its fellow, while keeping her eyes resolutely lowered.

Would the sandals come towards her, or go away again?

She could not remain kneeling on the floor forever. The subservient position rasped at her already raw pride, but the effort to rise to her feet proved to be too much for her suddenly weak leg muscles, so she compromised and sat back on her heels, pretending to be absorbed in checking the two pages to see which of them came first, as the only excuse that remained to her not to look up.

The silence in the room became total. Even the noises coming from the forest outside stopped, as if they, too, held their breath and waited.

For what?

Judi could not go on pretending to check the papers. She risked a peep round the edge of them, and as if motivated by her own slight movement the sandals moved as well. They took a step towards her, and Judi jerked the papers in front of her like a shield; the sandals paused, and an endless second later they spun away and strode off in the direction of the second bedroom.

As Nick passed by Judi, he flung harshly at her down-bent head, 'Why don't you try holding the papers the right way up? The words might make more sense to you if they weren't upside-down.'

The violent trembling which seized her made no sense at all, and the strong penstrokes became a blur in front of her eyes as the door closed behind Nick. She used the edge of the table to pull herself upright and collapsed on to the chair standing ready in front of the typewriter.

The forest noises flowed softly back again, as if the inhabitants of the night had let out a collective sigh, and Judi's breath exploded through her tight lips to join them, as she smoothed out the two sheets of paper, becoming conscious for the first time that her clenched fingers were crushing them into an unreadable ball.

Nick must have seen the convulsive tightening of her fists, and known himself to be the cause, and Judi's pride recoiled from the inference he must have drawn from her action. To erase its effect, she drove shaking fingers to the typewriter keys, blinked her eyes clear of the fog which persisted in drifting between them and the papers, and tapped out a defiant denial of her shaken nerves, which she hoped would register with Nick through the thin bamboo walls that separated them, and convince him that she did not care.

For his opinion, or for him? How accurate was Dave's guess at the real motivation behind her behaviour tonight?

The unanswerable questions drove her to a frenzy of effort, although her weary mind was unable to take in any of the content of the pages, and she was no wiser about what she had typed when, two hours later, she finally clipped the last sheet to the pile and passed a hand wearily across her aching forehead.

'Have you finished?' Nick wanted to know.

He stood beside her with a manila folder in his hand, and Judi looked at it with disbelief. 'Not more work?' she groaned. Surely he did not expect her to continue to type all night? Even for Nick, that was going too far. A quick glance at her watch showed that the hands stood at two minutes past midnight, and goaded beyond endurance she flared, 'I charge double-time after midnight.'

'For what?' Nick taunted.

His hand came out and fielded Judi's furious fist, split seconds before it connected with his cheek.

'You little jungle cat,' he grated. 'But the jungle doesn't frighten me.'

He was a part of it himself. Part of the mysterious, primeval life that stalked, and pounced, and throbbed, outside the windows of the frail cabin, and fear as dark as the forest itself invaded Judi as Nick's mouth implanted itself upon her quivering lips.

She could not speak. Her dazed mind was unable to think. And Nick's arms trapped hers against her sides, so that she was unable to move.

She could only feel.

The fury of Nick's kiss sucked the well of her feelings dry. It exposed every raw nerve-ending to an agonised awareness of him, as he moulded her tightly against his hard length, crushing her to him with a strength she could not gainsay, which borrowed its ferocity from the teeming life in the forest beyond the walls.

It lashed her for forgetting that her sole reason for being on the trip at all was to do his work, and his alone, and punished her for kissing Dave.

The hard edge of the table cutting into her back felt kindly in comparison with the implacable steel rods of Nick's arms and, unable to move her own, Judi twisted her head frantically from side to side to try to free her lips from his.

As ineffectually as a linnet might beat its wings against the bars of a cage. Her strength was no match for Nick, and a tiny moan broke from her lips as she felt her senses begin to slip.

Slight though the sound was, Nick's alert ears caught it, and his arms slackened their hold slightly, although they still remained round her, trapping her in their circle while his tongue flicked across the bruised line of her lips, stinging them to pulsating life.

Desperately she fought him, and her eyes as they stared up into his rock-hard face grew wild as it dawned upon her that she was fighting herself as well.

She loathed Nick for what he was doing to her, while a crazy, completely irrational part of her longed to abandon herself to the unnameable sensations exploding within her which demanded she meet Nick kiss for kiss, with a passion to match his own.

Except that Nick's passion sprang from fury, and not desire.

The reminder acted like a douche of icy water on the fire flaring inside Judi. With a convulsive wriggle she freed her arms, and beat against Nick's broad chest with doubled fists, trying to force him to free her. With a quick wrench of her head she managed to free her lips, and hissed through them furiously, 'Loose me, or I'll scream for help.'

'Who to? Dave?' Nick jeered, and loosed a virago inside Judi instead, which she had never suspected might hide within her erstwhile gentle self. With an ejaculation of rage, she struck out with fists and feet, and with a muttered curse Nick let her go. She fell back across the desk, temporarily off balanced by the fury of her momentum.

Her flailing hands came into contact with the pile of papers which she had just finished typing, and she scooped up the bundle, flung them at Nick, and shouted, 'If you want any more typing done tonight, do it yourself.'

With an agile swerve she ducked under the hand he put out to detain her, and fled for the bedroom door. Panting, she pushed it shut behind her and leaned against its light bamboo slats, and shook from head to foot, while she thanked her lucky stars that Pet was noisily asleep in the next bed, lying on her back and snoring through slack lips, completely oblivious of the drama.

Over the rhythmic noise, Judi's sensitised ears followed the slight sounds of Nick's movements from the other room. A light tapping sound told her that the papers she had thrown at him were being reduced to order, and then a softer, sighing noise placed the manila folder round them; agonised seconds later, she heard the second bedroom door open and close.

Reaction set in, and Judi went limp. It felt as if every joint of her body suddenly gave way, like a puppet that had its strings unexpectedly cut, and she staggered like a drunken creature as she groped the short distance from the door to her bed.

The edge of it caught against her shins and brought her to an abrupt halt, and her knees finally folded, and deposited her in a crumpled heap on top of the covers.

She could not tell how long she lay there, shivering in spite of the humid heat, while she tried in vain to come to terms with the knowledge that, while Nick's kisses had been activated by fury and not desire, the feelings they had aroused within herself went beyond desire.

To what?

Harsh sobs racked her shaking body, and she turned her face into the pillow, as much to hide it from the inevitable answer as to stifle the anguish that it brought, so that Pet should not wake up and witness her humiliation.

CHAPTER SIX

WHEN Judi woke the next morning, she thought her watch had stopped.

She shook it. Ten-thirty? Surely not. And then she remembered that she had checked it at midnight when Nick had brought in the folder, and the hands had shown the correct time then.

Shaken, she leapt out of bed. A glance showed her that Pet's bed was already made, and its owner nowhere to be seen. Judi showered and dressed at record speed, and reflected as she stroked a hasty brush through her hair in front of the dressing-table mirror that perhaps it was as well that Pet was already gone.

In the light from the window, the looking-glass reflected clear evidence of the storm of the night before, and she frowned. Pride would not allow her to confront Nick with reddened lids. His eyes were all-seeing, and she refused to give him the satisfaction of knowing that he had made her cry.

How to cover up the ravages presented a problem. Judi did not use make-up herself, and she wrinkled her nose in fastidious distaste at the sight of the heavy pancake-type powder which Pet had left untidily on the dressing-table-top. If she borrowed some of that, her amateur efforts would be bound to show, and merely draw attention to what she was trying to cover up.

Her eyes stared back at her from the mirror, clouded pools in her white face, still carrying the shadows of the wild weeping of the night before. She sighed wearily. She felt drained, and she wondered how she would be able to summon sufficient energy to meet Nick's unrelenting demands during the day.

Her sunglasses suggested a more acceptable form of disguise for the state of her eyes, and she tucked them into the top pocket of her bush shirt, ready to slip on.

The cabin was silent. She opened the bedroom door and cautiously surveyed the empty living-room. Nick had probably left in a huff when she had not appeared for breakfast, which meant she was likely to get the sack from her job on his return.

She shrugged, and muttered, 'I don't care if he does sack me,' although she knew that she did, and her spirits plummeted as she ventured in search of a much-needed cup of coffee.

The kitchen was as empty as the living-room, and after listening carefully Judi could detect no sound to indicate that the others were still around. Her lips twisted. Pet had got her wish, and was no doubt now accompanying Nick on his photographic forays.

Unaccountably the picture of them together hurt, and Judi spooned extra coffee into her cup to ward off the pain, as the kettle began to bubble a warning from the stove.

'Make that two while you're about it,' a voice commanded from the door. 'I could use a coffee myself.'

Nick! Judi jumped violently, and poured the water over the table instead of into her cup.

'I thought you'd gone,' she blurted, not knowing which to grab at first—a mopping-up cloth or her scattered wits.

'I'll take that, before you scald yourself.'

Nick removed the kettle from her nerveless fingers while she hurriedly wiped up the spill. He directed a jet of boiling water into Judi's cup, and made another coffee for himself, and his alert glance absorbed the soupy darkness of the cup which Judi had prepared for herself as he pushed it towards her. Taking his own, he lowered himself negligently on to a corner of the table, and said, 'I was waiting for you to wake up and come with me.'

Judi stiffened defensively. 'It was your fault I over-slept. You shouldn't have kept me working until after midnight.'

Belatedly, she remembered the tell-tale signs of dis-tress marking her face, and she snatched the sun-glasses out of her pocket, and slid them on to her nose, uncomfortably aware of Nick's keen glance reading what she did not want him to see.

The steam from the coffee-cup promptly blanked out the lens, and she made a face as she sipped the ultra-strong brew. Nick said, 'Have some more milk in it.'

Nothing missed his eyes, but Judi's own were ren-dered temporarily inactive. She heard him push the milk container across the table towards her, but the steamy lenses prevented her from being able to locate its exact whereabouts, and she fumbled, refusing to remove the sunglasses and betray her weakness.

'Allow me,' Nick said drily, and, reaching out, he steadied her hand that held the cup, while he picked up the milk and reduced the coffee to a more agreeable colour, then risked its very existence when he released her fingers, for they trembled so much from his touch that they sent the coffee spilling over the rim into the saucer.

He answered her accusation blandly, 'That's why I allowed you to sleep overtime, in lieu.'

He had not forgotten her taunt of the night before, and Judi's lips tightened, remembering what his reply had been. She sidetracked hurriedly. 'Where are Pet and Dave?'

'They've gone to play golf.'

'There's no need to be sarcastic.' She was still vulnerable, and in spite of her resolution his sharpness hurt, and she blinked hurriedly to cover the warning prick behind her eyes.

'It isn't sarcasm. Just plain truth. Golf is big business out here.'

'A golf course, out here in the mountains?'

'Surprising, isn't it? I didn't believe it the first time, either, but it's a fact. There's an eighteen-hole course not very far away, and Dave wanted to try it out on behalf of his firm's clients. That was his excuse, anyway.'

Nick seemed to hesitate before he added, in an expressionless voice, 'You can go and join them, if you want to.'

'No, thanks. I don't play golf. I've always considered it to be the quickest way to spoil a good walk.'

If Nick wanted to play, then good riddance. It would give her an hour or two on her own in which to recover, and by the time he returned she would have her jangled nerves under better control.

Nick nodded, and destroyed her wishful thinking with, 'My view exactly. Which is why I've decided we'll take the day off as well, and explore at our leisure for a change.'

'What about the papers you had in that manila folder last night? They'll have to be typed.' Judi clutched at the only escape route which presented itself.

'There wasn't anything in the folder. I only brought it in to cover the papers you had piled on the table.'

The papers she had thrown at him. After all that, the folder had been empty, and her battle with Nick need never have started! Judi stared at him, wide-eyed, torn between a desire to laugh at the bitter irony of it all, and an even more urgent desire to weep at the waste. She put her cup and saucer down carefully on to the table-top and started with difficulty, 'Nick, I...'

Nick rose to his full height, and took a step towards her. 'Judi, I...'

They both stopped, and laughter won; Nick took a second, swift stride that carried him round the table, and Judi was in his arms, with her head tipped back so that she had a clear view of the pulse-stirring cleft in his chin for a sweet, brief second before his lips came down to claim her mouth.

He groaned between kisses, 'Judi, you're beautiful. Beautiful. And I love you. I made you cry. Will you ever forgive me?'

Gently he removed the sunglasses and kissed her swollen lids, and the touch of his lips was a magic potion that made her murmured, 'It doesn't matter now,' wholly true.

A surging happiness swept through her like a tidal wave, carrying her along on its crest, and leaving behind all the darkness, the tears and the uncertainty which had so plagued her.

She had come to Thailand hoping to learn what it was she wanted from life, and now she knew.

She wanted Nick. And, miraculously, he wanted her.

Judi raised her arms as far as she could reach and circled them round his neck, then, tipping up her face, she sweetly returned kiss for kiss.

'Judi...' His voice was hoarse as he crushed her to him, with all the passion, but none of the anger, of the night before, and now she had no desire to fight herself free.

'Judi...'

'Here are your car keys, Professor. I've parked the jeep you ordered, just outside. I'd be glad of a lift back to the garage, if you're going that way.'

Nick muttered as he straightened, and Judi giggled, her eyes dancing at his look of frustration, and she mouthed to him silently, 'It doesn't matter. Later...'

Nothing mattered now. She loved Nick, and he loved her, and they had all the rest of their lives for their love to grow in, so what did a few more hours of waiting matter?

Nick called out, 'We're in the kitchen,' and a slender, olive-skinned man wearing the engaging Thai smile appeared through the doorway and handed over a set of ignition keys.

'One of the trucks has broken down, and the other jeep that should have trailed me here has had to go out to the driver with spares.' That explained his request for a lift. 'Of course, if it isn't convenient...' His look rested understandingly upon Judi.

'It's convenient,' Nick assured him. 'Though I was hoping to persuade Judi to have something to eat before we go out. She hasn't had any breakfast.'

'It isn't good to go sightseeing on an empty stomach,' their visitor admonished. Then he confessed ruefully, 'Although I didn't stop for food either this morning, what with the truck breaking down and the generator blowing up. *Mai pen rai.*'

He shrugged philosophically, and Judi invited, 'Have some now, with me. What about you, Nick? Have you had any breakfast?'

'No, but I will now.'

It was a merry meal. The garage man initiated Judi into the mysteries of preparing a stir-fry, while Nick searched out bread and plates and made more coffee, and Judi wondered if his lack of breakfast meant that he had overslept, too.

An hour later they dropped their still smiling companion at his place of work, and Nick promised, 'I'll arrange for the guide to return the jeep to you as soon as we get back from the safari tomorrow morning.'

'What safari?' Judi wanted to know curiously as they started off again, with Nick driving this time.

'A night safari. I meant to tell you. It's why we're having the day off today. We start after dark this evening, and travel through the forest to the various water-holes in the hope of seeing the animals when they come to drink. It's a popular attraction with the tourists.'

Dave had said the forest came alive at night, and a thrill of anticipation ran through Judi at the prospect of being a part of it with Nick. He continued, 'We'll explore this morning and sleep this afternoon, then work from dark to dawn. I won't forget to pay you double time after midnight,' he told her gravely, and she laughed.

'I might let you off paying, if the views are worth it.' She asked belatedly, 'Will Pet and Dave be coming, too?' and crossed her fingers in the secrecy of her pockets, waiting for Nick's reply.

'No, after a day of golf they won't feel like being up all night as well. Does it worry you?'

His eyes teased her lack of a chaperon, and Judi uncrossed her fingers, shook her head and threw back pertly, 'Not if it doesn't worry you,' and thrilled again to his tawny look that made Pet and Dave redundant, and even the guide an obligatory part of the entourage that he would have preferred to do without.

With the help of the nippy little jeep to transport them without effort from place to place, Nick threaded each magic moment of the morning on to a shining bead-string of experiences for Judi.

They took to their feet to climb up three hundred steps to visit a high-standing temple, and Judi pitied the monks as she rested beside one of the seven-headed serpents flanking the stairway, while Nick wielded his camera.

He tried to coax her to give up halfway, fearing that she might tire herself too much, but Judi insisted upon continuing with him to the top. Her energy seemed inexhaustible, and the way she felt now she was impervious to such minor physical discomforts as tiredness and hunger.

Even the heat did not seem to affect her today, but perhaps that was because Nick bought her an oiled paper umbrella, painted in bright butterflies to match her fan, and held it over her to shelter her from the sun.

The painted parasols, opened and set out to dry, turned the street into a kaleidoscope of colour, and Nick set Judi among them and took more pictures. When she asked, 'What about the captions to go with them?' he said firmly,

'You're having the day off. I can remember all that's necessary, and I'll dictate it to you when we get home.' And she thrilled anew, because home to Nick would one day mean the same to her.

She wrinkled her nose in disgust at the red-stained mouth of a trader selling carved bowls, and Nick said, *sotto voce*, 'He's chewing betel nut. It's an unlovely habit, but it's no worse than smoking.'

Pet smoked heavily, and Judi wondered fleetingly if the habit was another symptom of her insecurity, like overeating, and agreed without demur when Nick drew her past the stall with a cautionary, 'If you want a bowl, buy it from a reputable trader. Those are probably made from green teak, and they'll split in a month or two, when you're safely out of reach of returning them.'

It was the same when she was tempted by colourful lengths of silk on display at a market stall. Nick said, 'I'll take you to Jim Thompson's when we get back to Bangkok. You'll have all the choice of top-of-the-market silk there which you've ever dreamed of.'

She still hesitated, and argued doubtfully, 'What if there isn't time?'

Nick promised with a smile, 'I'll make time,' and she was content to leave it at that.

The rhythmic hammering of silversmiths attracted them to watch craftsmen, squatting at work under the shade of their shop blinds. They paused to admire intricate lacquerware, and mourned that luggage restrictions would not allow them to carry back examples of a potter's work to grace a terrace in faraway Shropshire.

After a meal, Nick drove them back to the cabin, shaking his head at Judi's protest that she could go on forever.

'You may feel like that now. But if you don't sleep this afternoon, you'll be too tired to take in anything that you see on the safari tonight.'

The wisdom of his advice was to prove itself before the safari was over, and Judi knew the night would live in her memory forever.

To her surprise, she slept soundly for the whole of the afternoon, although Nick's lingering kiss, and his gruff, 'Go, while I've still got enough strength to let you go alone,' sent her to bed with her heart doing crazy antics in her breast, which she was convinced would make sleep impossible.

Their guide was deep in conversation with Nick when she emerged, yawning, and the man's presence prevented any personal conversation between herself and Nick as they all ate again briefly, and the two men planned their route on a map spread out on the table between them.

Pet and Dave came back just as they were ready to start out. Judi longed to ask Dave how he had fared. Pet looked subdued, she thought, but she felt heartened by Dave's cheerful wink as he passed her on the veranda steps on his way into the cabin.

And then she forgot Dave and Pet, and tucked herself in beside Nick on the back seat of the jeep. Her eyes danced at his murmured, 'If you sit too close, I'm liable to forget what I'm here for, and hold you on my knee, instead of my camera.'

'If I distract you so much, why don't you sit in the front, beside the driver?' she asked him demurely.

'You'd distract a block of marble,' he growled back, but he made no attempt to do as she suggested, and went on in answer to her question, 'Watch out for wild elephants, deer, wild boar... if we're lucky, we might even spot a tiger. But no, I'm afraid there aren't any lions.'

Judi's chuckle was a soft merriment that brought his head round swiftly in the darkness. 'If Dave's to be believed, there's a lion in the car with me.'

Nick snorted. 'Dave and his astrology!' Then he slanted her an oblique look that sent a delicious shiver through her, and allowed, 'Maybe there's something in what he says, after all,' making it a close, personal thing that bound them together.

The track climbed high, and forest closed round them, its thick canopy a protective umbrella which excluded any light from the sky; darkness wrapped them in a precious privacy in the back seat of the vehicle, cutting them off from the driver and from the forward-raking beams of the vehicle's headlights, which turned the huge trunks of the teak trees into ghostly sentinels guarding who knew what secrets in the undergrowth on either side of the track.

Eyes glowed, fluorescent in the shadows, silently monitoring their progress, and once the jeep slowed to a crawl, and Judi turned up a questioning face to Nick. He bent his head and put his lips to her ear, and she felt the light zephyr of his breath against her cheek as he whispered, 'Wild elephant. Don't talk. Just look in the direction I point.'

His arm cradled her reassuringly against him, while his finger pointed out dark shapes standing motionless among the trees, only feet away from them, that Judi's unaccustomed eyes would otherwise have missed.

Soon afterwards, a gleam of water ahead borrowed faint light from a gap in the trees, and the driver brought the jeep to a halt. A more solid darkness than the leaf canopy just ahead revealed itself as a large, open-sided hut on stilts, built facing the water, which on closer inspection Judi saw was a pool made by the widening bend of a stream.

The guide left them and promptly began to mount the high flight of steps leading up to the hut, and Nick explained his apparent desertion with a low-voiced, 'He's making sure there are no four-footed visitors there before us.'

Judi shivered. She could not tell whether Nick was teasing or not, and it was too dark for her to be able to read his expression, but his arm made a safe circle round her, and at a signal from the guide she mounted the steps beside him confidently enough.

'There aren't so many steps this time.' She smiled, remembering the three hundred up to the temple that morning, and Nick admonished, 'Ssh. If you talk, the animals won't come.'

He dusted off a bench seat for her to sit on, where she had a clear view over the pool, and went to lean against the veranda rail himself, with his camera at the ready, where he waited without moving. Judi tried to occupy her mind with identifying the subdued squeaks and grunts and scuffles that came from sources which she was unable to see, an impossible task with Nick so close a magnet for her eyes.

Soon, the noise-makers began to identify themselves as they crept from their hiding-places and came to slake their thirst at the water's edge, and Judi watched, electrified, as a huge striped cat slunk from the undergrowth to join them, and marvelled that they did not all run for their lives instead of merely edging away to a safe distance, and keeping a wary eye on the big male tiger as it drank its fill, then left them unharmed when it melted back into the thickets.

Muffled mechanical clicks told her that Nick was getting the shots he wanted, and then from somewhere a bird screeched; startled, Judi forgot the need for silence, and exclaimed, 'That sounded just like a barnyard cockerel.'

'That's exactly what it was,' Nick answered, and straightened up. 'There's a hill village close by, attached to a logging camp. It's time we were on our way, if you want to see the working elephants have their morning bath.'

They paused to watch the sun rise first.

The track led them out of the forest, across a high, rocky escarpment, and at a word from Nick the driver stopped the jeep, and Nick urged Judi, 'Come and watch the dawn with me. It's worth seeing.'

There would be other days, and other dawns, but surely never another dawn like this one. Nick lifted her down to stand beside him, and together they climbed uphill to a rocky outcrop that seemed to Judi to be like the end of the world.

A wide valley fell away at their feet, and an endless expanse of sky lay in front of them, like a empty canvas awaiting the master-strokes of the Supreme Artist, that came as they watched in pale washes of silver and gold, and then warmed the waiting world with a final, dazzling rose.

'It's magic,' Judi whispered, awed.

Nick turned her in his arms, and bending his head he pressed his lips on to her mouth, and it was like the final bars of a lovely overture when he murmured, 'And I'm bewitched. I love you, Judi.'

'And I love you.'

Their lips met and fused while, unheeded, the sun rose above them like a benediction, into an azure sky. Long minutes later, they walked back down the hill again, and the guide took them on to the higher reaches of the river where the *mahouts* from the logging-camp were giving their trained working elephants their morning bath.

Judi laughed at the animals' clumsy enjoyment of the daily ritual, and at the smiling invitation of one of the *mahouts* she helped to scrub the nearest animal, while Nick took photographs of her amateur efforts, and her heart knew at last what it was to be fulfilled.

The next few days passed in a rosy haze for Judi. True to his promise, Nick took her to Jim Thompson's, where she was spoilt for choice from the dazzling display of silk material on offer at the store.

Nick wandered away among the counters while she hesitated over buying this or that, but returned in time to translate *bahts* into pounds sterling, and give her some idea of the worth of her purchases, teasing her indulgently when she insisted upon carrying her parcel with her instead of leaving it to be delivered to the hotel.

Love gave her an inner glow, and each new sight and sound took on an extra dimension because Nick loved her. He never tired of telling her so, and when Pet and Dave were with them, and he had perforce to restrain his ardour, his eyes constantly signalled his feelings. Judi was blissfully content, made doubly so when Dave confided, while Pet was far enough away not to overhear, 'I think I'm winning, Judi. I still owe you for that.'

'My pleasure,' Judi smiled.

She hugged her own secret to her for a little while longer. It was still too new and too precious to be shared with the world at large, and it was still intact on their last day, before the evening flight that was to take them back to England.

Nick said, 'We've done all we can now. Let's spend the rest of the day on the beach.'

If Judi was disappointed that his invitation included Pet and Dave, she hid her feelings, collected her swimsuit, and sat beside Nick in the hired car while he drove south in search of a good spot from which to bathe.

Pet made no demur as Dave helped her into the back seat beside him, and Judi noticed, startled, that Pet's dress did not fit nearly so tightly as when she had first met the older woman.

In spite of her still considerable bulk, Pet proved to be an agile swimmer, and the four of them spent a blissful few hours lazily exploring hidden lagoons among tiny, offshore islets, the clear green depths dotted with coral, and alive with brilliantly coloured fish.

They raced each other ashore, and dried off on the sand, and afterwards Nick drove them to Pattaya for lunch, where they feasted off lobster and other exotic fish which were strange to Judi, but which tasted delicious.

She noticed that Pet ate sparingly, and for the first time since they had met the older woman forbore to light a cigarette as soon as she'd finished her meal.

Dave must be getting through to Pet at last, Judi reflected. What else could make such a difference in a
person, in so short a time, except love?

She could not see the luminous quality of her own
eyes as they lingered on Nick, as if a lamp had been
lit, in their velvet depths, that burned only for him,
and when he rose and paid the bill, and said, 'That's
it, team. End of journey,' she had no regrets, because
her journey at Nick's side was only just beginning.

Back at the hotel, she hesitated about wiring her
parents to warn them of her return, and decided
against it. It was better not to give them time to prime
their guns for the battle which she knew was inevitable when she split with Robert.

Much better to arrive unheralded and take them all
by surprise, and then, when she had given Robert back
his ring, Nick would call to collect her the following
day, and take her with him to Shropshire, away from
all the harassment and the fuss.

Nick did not know about Robert yet, but that was
not important. Judi refused to spoil their time in
Thailand together. She wanted to remember it unsul-
lied by other problems. She would tell him about
Robert on the plane, and his support would give her
the courage for the coming ordeal that did not seem
to be nearly such an ordeal now as when she had first
left home.

The packing was done, and there began the period
of suspended animation which is the *bête noire* of
every traveller, the endless, dragging time between
having everything ready and actually starting out.

Dinner was over, the taxi to take them to the airport
was not due for another hour and a half. Dave and
Pet sat together in one of the lounges, and after a

quick peep inside Judi decided against joining them. They seemed to be totally absorbed in whatever they were talking about and, having given Dave the necessary push into courtship, she had no wish to disrupt its progress now.

The lift gates slid open into the foyer, and a porter appeared with her case, and three others that presumably belonged to the rest of the team, and wheeled them to a waiting area just inside the main doors.

Judi strolled across to the reception desk to hand in her room-key. She would not need it now that her luggage had been collected. Nick was at the desk when she got there. He looked up and smiled as she approached, then turned to reply to something the receptionist said to him before continuing to deal with the paperwork that was claiming his attention when Judi arrived.

'Here's your engagement ring, Miss Bartlett,' the receptionist smiled. 'It wouldn't do to leave that behind, would it?'

Judi frowned. She would dearly love to leave the ring behind. It was an unwanted reminder of the battles that faced her when she returned home, and she took it reluctantly from the receptionist, who requested her politely to, 'Sign here for it, please.'

Judi did not want to wear the ring again, but she supposed that it would be safer on her finger than if she put it in her handbag. It would be an impossible complication if she were to lose it and had nothing to return to Robert when she reached home.

He would never believe that she had not sold it. It was going to be difficult enough to convince a man of his overwhelming conceit that she did not want to marry him, and his wealth.

With a nod of thanks, she slipped the jewel in place on her finger, signed the receipt, and straightened up from the desk to find Nick staring at her as if he had never seen her before.

His face had a curiously white tinge under his tan, but perhaps that was the unnatural effect of the fluorescent lighting which kept at bay the inky darkness of the Eastern night.

'Did the receptionist say, an *engagement ring*?'

Nick took her by the arm in a grip that made dents in Judi's soft flesh, and she winced as he propelled her roughly into a small anteroom off the main foyer, out of earshot of the desk staff.

'Nick, let go of me,' she cried. 'You're hurting.'

'Answer me,' he gritted, still holding on. 'Did she say, an engagement ring?'

'Yes, it is. Although, in a way, it isn't...' In her confusion, Judi stammered incoherently. 'I was going to explain to you about it, when we're on the plane.'

'Engagement rings don't need any explanation. They're self-evident.'

Nick's voice was a snarl, and he released her arm, and grasped her left hand instead, bringing up her fingers in a crushing hold that raised the ring high, and held it like an accusation between them.

'Another man's ring,' he growled. 'All this time, you've been stringing me along. What a fool you must have thought me.'

'Nick, it isn't like that. I told you, I was going to explain.'

'This is all the explanation I need.' He tossed her hand away as if he loathed its touch, when just a few short hours ago he could not seem to hold it enough.

'I should have known better, after watching your performance with Dave at the cabin.'

'That's all it was, just a performance.' Shock and bewilderment reduced Judi's voice to a whisper.

'If it was, then you're a first-class actress.'

'Nick, listen to me. There *is* an explanation.'

'There are a good many things that need explaining. You probably thought I wouldn't find out. Well, now I have, and I don't want to listen to your lies. Dave said it all the other day, when he told you he still owed you—for what you said was a pleasure,' he grated, and Judi blanched at the savage glitter in his eyes. 'Did you charge him double-time, too? Or did you enjoy it so much that you waived the charge?'

'You beast!'

Anger flooded through Judi, rising to match Nick's anger, and her voice spat outrage at his insult.

'How dare you?' she shrilled.

'I dare because it's true. Don't try to deny it. I heard Dave speak those very words to you. I suppose you thought I was safely out of earshot, the same as Pet? What a dance you've led me. But the music has stopped now, although I suppose you'll find another toy to play with soon enough. To girls like you, it all comes under the heading of *snuk*.'

The happy Thai word for innocent pleasure came hurling from his tight lips like a bullet, aimed to wound. His tone gave its meaning a very different connotation, and Judi's colour receded, leaving her cheeks resembling parchment, but, before she could draw breath to retort, Nick rushed on, 'So far as I'm concerned, it's journey's end for you and me, as well. No doubt you'll get a good laugh over your souvenirs when you show them to your fiancé. It would be interesting to know how much you tell him about your activities in Thailand.'

'If that's what you think of me, you can have all the souvenirs back. The chopsticks, and the fan, and the parasol.'

Nick gave a bitter laugh. 'The painted butterflies on them were an excellent choice. That exactly describes what you are. A butterfly, flitting from one man to the other. First your fiancé, then Dave, and then me. How many more besides? What does it feel like, to be anybody's woman?'

Judi longed to strike his hard, sneering face. She knew an uncivilised urge to scream and kick and scratch, and instead felt a humiliating faintness take hold of her. A loud roaring sounded in her ears, and she swayed, and through a growing darkness she heard her own voice cry hoarsely, 'The very second I get home, I'll post them all back to you, then you can have a laugh instead at your lucky escape. If I can't find your home address, I'll send them to the travel firm. They'll send them on.'

'You'll be coming to my home address, so you can bring them with you.'

'After what you've just said to me, you must be mad if you think . . .'

'You'll stick by your agreement to complete the job you started, if I have to drag you to Shropshire.'

'You can't force me to do your work.'

'I'll make you pay dear if you refuse. The newspapers are always interested in getting an article or two from my trips abroad, and I'm sure the Sunday tabloids would love what I could tell them about you. I don't imagine your fiancé, or your family, would enjoy reading what they made of the activities of my stand-in secretary.'

'You wouldn't dare.'

'Try me. You've got plenty of time to decide what to do. We don't land at Heathrow until about noon tomorrow, and in case you've conveniently forgotten, our arrangement was that I should pick you up from your home at two o'clock on the following day, to drive to Shropshire. That should give you a whole night in which to console your fiancé for your further absence.'

Judi's pent-up breath hissed through her clenched teeth like the sound of a furious cat.

'I don't have to stand here and take these insults from you. You're completely out of your mind. And as for the plane getting into Heathrow tomorrow, your flight will, but mine won't. After this, I refuse to fly anywhere with you.'

Rage helped her out of the hotel doorway at a pace she would not have been capable of otherwise. She heard Nick shout, 'Judi...' behind her, but she ignored his command and fled on, retaining sufficient presence of mind to give the heavy swing doors a hearty push on her way out, making them swing round behind her at a speed that would effectively prevent Nick from using them for the few vital seconds it would take to effect her escape.

Once outside, she dodged into the first side street she came to, and ran blindly, grateful for the darkness that hid her fleeing figure.

She knew that the shops remained open until fairly late, and she had noticed a number of travel agents on her journeys around the city with Nick. She would go into the first one she came to and get her return flight changed, she did not care to when, so long as she did not have to endure another minute of Nick's company.

Several twists and turns later, to make sure she had completely shaken Nick from her trail if he did try to pursue her, a painful stitch in her side slowed her headlong rush to a jerky walk, and her reduced speed allowed her more time in which to take notice of her surroundings.

She peered round her, and the first twinges of uneasiness gripped her. There were no shops, travel or otherwise, in sight. For the first time, she noticed the complete absence of brightly lit window displays.

She appeared to be in an alley of some kind, and it was narrow and dark. Her clothes clung to her, damp with perspiration from her running, but in spite of that she felt herself go suddenly icy cold. In her haste to get away from Nick, she had taken no account of the direction in which she'd run.

Now, she realised with a frightened shiver, she was hopelessly lost.

Somehow, she must find her way back to the main thoroughfare. But how? And did she turn right, or left, or go straight on?

The twists and turns she had taken so heedlessly had completely disorientated her, and she felt suddenly drained of strength, as much by the shock of discovering her position as by her exertions. She stumbled forward, praying that the next turning might reveal some clue as to her whereabouts.

Her appearance, alone in the alley, drew speculative looks from the few pedestrians she met, but she kept her face averted and hurried on. It would be pointless for her to try to ask the way. She spoke no

Thai, and she remembered Nick saying that English was not widely used. She also remembered, with another shiver, that an approach from a woman alone, after dark, might be misinterpreted.

And then her courage returned as she recalled something else. The hotel card. That small piece of pasteboard which Nick had insisted she keep safely in her shoulder-bag, and which she had so resented having to carry. It could prove to be her lifeline now.

A crossroads loomed ahead, and the street at the junction was wider and better lit than the one she had just come along. It contained cars. And a cab. The cab was coming in her direction.

Frantically Judi fumbled at the zip of her shoulder-bag. Her haste jammed the delicate mechanism, and she shook it backwards and forwards furiously, willing it to work. She must get the card out, and stop the driver of the vehicle before he went past.

Just when she was on the point of desperation, the zip gave way to her tug, and she grabbed the precious piece of pasteboard and waved it in front of the cab.

Judi could have sobbed with relief when the vehicle slowed. Her legs felt weak, but she forced them to hold her and take her towards the driver's open window, to show him the card. She was within inches of him reading it, when the rear door of the cab opened, and two hands reached out and grabbed her, and pulled her unceremoniously inside.

She opened her mouth to scream, and a hard hand closed over it, cutting off the sound.

'Be quiet, and stop struggling,' Nick's voice commanded her harshly.

It cut through Judi's terror like a knife. An overwhelming sense of relief flooded over her and momentarily threatened her senses, but the faintness passed when Nick heaved her up on to the seat beside him and held on to her with a vice-like grip.

'Just in case you're insane enough to try to take off again,' he growled. 'Thanks to you, we're all likely to miss our flight. We've got about ten minutes flat to get to the airport.'

The pain of his grip stung Judi back to life again. She gasped, 'I won't fly with you.'

'How do you propose to get back home, if you don't?'

'There are other flights.'

'Not for three weeks. The conference in Bangkok ended today, and there are hundreds of delegates with open-ended flight tickets, all wanting to get on the first available plane out.'

'I'd rather wait three weeks than——'

Nick sliced through her objections. 'It wouldn't bother me if you waited three months, or forever. But you either fly home with the team, or start explaining yourself to the Thai authorities. In case you'd forgotten, your visa runs out tomorrow. So keep your fingers crossed that we can make it to the airport in time.'

CHAPTER SEVEN

AFTER fourteen of the most miserable hours that Judi had ever spent, they touched down at Heathrow.

They had caught the plane by a hair's breadth. Only Nick's fluency in the Thai language cleared a passage for them among the teeming crowds at the airport, and got them through the formalities and into the departure lounge brief minutes before the plane was due to take off.

Nick pushed Judi down on to her seat and buckled the seat-belt round her as if he could not trust her, even then, not to try to run away again. That done, he finally let go of her arm, and Judi rubbed the red weals left by his relentless fingers, and flared resentfully, 'I'm going to sit somewhere else.'

Hemmed in between Nick and Pet, she could feel herself a target for their silent hostility from either side, and the prospect of enduring such an atmosphere for the next fourteen hours was more than she could bear.

'You'll sit in the seat allocated to you, and stop arguing,' Nick snapped. 'The plane's carrying a capacity load, so there aren't any empty seats you can go to, and you've already caused enough trouble for one day, without upsetting anyone else now.'

It was she, Judi, who should be the one to feel aggrieved, after the way Nick had spoken to her, but suddenly she felt too tired to fight any more. Reaction set in and she sagged back in her seat; the drone of the aircraft engines became an ebb and flow of noise in her ears, and she knew resignedly that a splitting headache was not many minutes away.

Her engagement ring felt like a leaden weight on her hand. She intercepted Pet's startled look, which passed from the ring to Nick and back again, but his closed expression did not encourage questions, and rather than become a target for the older woman's curiosity herself Judi closed her eyes and feigned sleep, and allowed Pet to make what she pleased of the presence of the jewel on her finger.

Unaware, her pretence became a reality, and she slipped from consciousness into oblivion as the events of the last few hours took their toll. She awoke a couple of hours later feeling refreshed, and as if she had just left a nightmare behind her.

She stretched and yawned, and wondered where the mechanical droning was coming from. She turned her head to find out, and looked up, straight into Nick's eyes, looking down at her.

Her eyes widened, and she sat upright abruptly. The nightmare was a reality, and still with her, a glance at her wristwatch said for many hours yet to come. The time seemed, to her ragged nerves, to stretch into an eternity, before the longed-for request to fasten all seat-belts appeared on the illuminated dial overhead, and soon afterwards she disembarked on home soil, with the feeling that she was being released from prison.

The moment she emerged from the terminal building, she realised with dismay that her sentence was only just beginning.

She passed unscathed through Customs, and hurried on without looking back. With luck, Nick might be stopped, and his luggage subjected to a random search, which would delay him for long enough to allow her to grab a taxi and be well clear of the airport before he got out himself.

She had already said goodbye to Dave and Pet. Dave kissed her, and Judi wondered if Nick could see them. Not that it made any difference now. His opinion of her could not be lower, and on the strength of it she kissed Dave back with more enthusiasm than she might otherwise have shown, as she whispered, 'Good luck,' and felt she could do with some of that commodity herself.

'I'll send you an invitation to the wedding when it happens,' Dave whispered back, and Judi smiled at the 'when', which revealed a confidence he had not shown before.

Pet's farewell was predictably cooler, but she returned Judi's wave as the two made their way to their car, and Judi hurried towards the taxi rank, having tactfully refused their offer of a lift.

Nick and a newspaper reporter caught up with her when she was only half-way to her objective. She rested her suitcase on the ground for a moment to ease her arm, and almost immediately a lean brown hand reached down and plucked it up again, and Nick said, 'I'll take that.'

Judi whirled on him. 'Put it down. I'm not coming with you. I'm taking a taxi.'

'*We're* taking a taxi,' he contradicted, and signalled one towards him. 'I'll drop you off at home. It will save time tomorrow, when I come to pick you up, if I know beforehand how to get to your house.'

He was unrelenting in his determination to make her finish the job she had started. A combination of jet lag and misery, and dread of the coming ordeal when she reached home, washed over Judi like a black wave, and she turned to Nick in a desperate appeal.

'Nick, I . . .'

'Well, Miss Bartlett, if this isn't a coincidence, bumping into you here. Where have you been hiding away all these weeks?' the news reporter pounced gleefully.

'I haven't been hiding. I've been . . . on holiday.'

Judi regarded the man with disfavour. He worked for one of the more sensational of the tabloids, and had been active at her engagement party, so it was pointless to make believe that he had mistaken her for someone else.

His alert look warned her that he had noticed her slight hesitation, and that it had honed his curiosity to an even sharper edge. Was it really by chance that he had turned up at the airport, just at this very moment, or . . . ? She said in a furious undertone to Nick, 'Is this your doing?'

He had threatened to talk to the newspapers, and he could not have chosen a better medium for printing malicious gossip than the unsavoury representative standing within a foot of her now.

'Not guilty,' Nick denied, equally low. 'As the man says, it's pure coincidence.'

Judi hated herself for believing him, and hated herself still more for not putting up a fight when Nick handed their cases to the taxi-driver, and, draping his arm round her shoulders, raised his voice so that the newsman could not help but hear him, as he said clearly, 'Get inside, or we'll be late home.'

Not 'you' but 'we', implying . . .

Judi's mind boggled at what the reporter must be inferring. If Nick had truly not been responsible for the man being here, he was not slow to take advantage of the presence of the Press to tighten his hold upon her.

'Some holiday,' the newsman laughed, and his insolent eyes roved in interested speculation from Judi to Nick. 'And some souvenir you've brought home with you,' he added, and his grin widened. 'I wonder if your fiancé will like him as much as you do.'

'You...' Judi gritted, and got no further. Nick's hands clamped hard on her shoulders, and he spun her round and propelled her through the door of the taxi before she could utter any of the other words that flooded to the end of her tongue.

He followed her inside, and slammed the door on the newsman's, 'He might have liked a stick of rock better,' and quick-wittedly the taxi-driver set the cab rolling, but not before the reporter had pushed his camera lens close against the window and a vivid flash warned Judi that her face, along with Nick's, would make headlines the next day.

Since the newsman was out of her reach she vented the full force of her wrath upon Nick.

'I hate you for this,' she hissed, and longed to strike him when he answered, unmoved,

'Hate away. I reckon you'll need all the fight you can muster when you reach home.'

Unexpectedly, he added, when the taxi drew up outside the house which was solid evidence of the prosperity of her father's stores, 'Do you want me to come in with you?'

Judi stared at him in total astonishment. 'If I had my way, I'd never see you again.'

His face tightened. A small muscle ticked at the corner of his jaw, and his voice was clipped, as if he had to force out the words as he retorted, 'In that case, you'd better shut your eyes when I call for you at two o'clock tomorrow afternoon.'

He was gone.

Judi stood on the driveway, with her suitcase beside her, and felt more lonely than she had ever been in her life before. Even the comfort of unburdening herself to Louise was denied to her, since her friend would still be away, helping to achieve her husband's ambition to walk as far as the Scottish borders during their holiday.

Judi felt bereft and defenceless, and irrationally she wanted Nick back beside her, no matter how cruel he had been.

Impulsively she spun round and ran back along the drive to the gateway, but the taxi-driver had been as quick off the mark as he had been at the airport, and she was in time only to see the blunt rear end of his vehicle disappear out of sight round a bend in the road.

Her feet dragged as she picked up her suitcase and walked back to the house, and inserted her key in the front door.

Alerted by the sight of the taxi, her parents appeared like jack-in-the-boxes in the front hall, and Judi braced herself for the storm.

'Where on earth have you been?' her mother shrilled without preamble.

'More to the point, who have you been with?' thundered her father.

Judi had expected a row, but this bid fair to turn into a full-scale war. She tried a placatory, 'I took the children home. I explained, in the note I left for you.'

'It doesn't take weeks to escort children back to their parents.'

'I know. I did explain in the note that I would stay on for a while afterwards, and have a holiday. I've done the same thing before, and it's never bothered you.'

'You weren't engaged to Robert before. We tried everywhere to get hold of you. The language school was closed for the holidays, and Louise had gone off to goodness knows where, gypsying about with that husband of hers, and the janitor didn't know where to find her either, let alone you.'

'Why the need to contact me? There wasn't anyone ill, was there?' Belated conscience stirred in Judi. Illness was something she had not considered when she'd escaped.

'Ill? Of course not. Why should anybody be ill?'

'Then why the urgency to get in touch with me? You haven't ever felt the need when I've extended my holidays before.'

In spite of herself, Judi's voice was bitter, but the reproach passed over the heads of her parents, and her mother rushed on accusingly, 'Didn't you give any thought at all to Robert, when you took off into the blue like that, alone? How must it appear to him, when you've only just got engaged? Your disappearance for so long without him, has caused all sorts of rumours to circulate. The Press have been prying about.'

In that case, one of their members had scored a scoop today, but Judi carefully kept that piece of information to herself. The uproar when the newspaper picture appeared in the morning would be quite bad enough, without adding to her problems now.

'Just because I'm engaged to Robert, it doesn't mean he owns me,' she flared.

Her father snapped back, 'Try telling that to Robert,' and reached for the telephone, with the evident intention of providing her with the opportunity.

Robert arrived soon afterwards, and his parents followed hot-foot on his heels, and now the odds were five against one, and Judi thought despairingly, if only I hadn't sent Nick away. He alone would have evened out the other four.

In vain she tried to explain the reasons for her action. In vain she pleaded with her own parents, at least, to listen to her side of the argument, and try to understand, and knew, even as she spoke, that she was wasting her breath.

Her mother complained, 'We arranged a dinner to celebrate the merger, and it caused speculation when you weren't there with Robert.'

Her father snapped, 'The shares have dropped a penny.'

'What have the shares got to do with Robert and me?'

'You know full well that the prices rose at the prospect of future security for the joint company, when you and Robert get married.'

It was always the same. The firm came before their own daughter. Judi's wavering self-control finally snapped, and grimly she hurled her bombshell.

'Robert and I won't be getting married.'

The stunned silence that followed her announcement was utter bliss, but it did not last for long. The storm broke about her head with renewed force.

Robert shouted, 'I knew it. I knew that escorting the children was just an excuse. Admit it. You've been with a man.'

Goaded beyond endurance, Judi shouted back, 'No I haven't. I've been with two.'

And, tugging off the hated ring, she did what she should have done months ago, and flung it back at him, then stormed up to her bedroom, where she locked herself in and resisted all demands that she must 'Come back downstairs again this instant, and see sense.'

She had only just come to her senses. She should have been strong and broken off her engagement to Robert when they had returned from India, but then she had been unsure. Then, she had not known what love really was, and now she did; and although it was too late, she still retained enough strength to refuse to accept second best.

It had to be Nick or nothing for her. And bleakly she looked at a future filled with nothing, and the prospect succeeded where all the recent recriminations had failed in soaking her pillow with tears.

The arrival of the newspaper the next morning, with an excellent picture of herself and Nick close together in the back of the taxi, refuelled the storm. Lily, the housekeeper, unashamedly read the rag, and Judi suspected that her mother borrowed it from time to time, although she would die rather than admit to reading such a down-market publication.

Unaware of the consternation she was creating, Lily brought in the missive with the breakfast toast. 'My, but it's a lovely picture of you, Miss Judi,' she beamed.

The caption underneath the picture read, 'Missing fiancée returns with another man. Is the mortar in the new brickwork already crumbling for the two High Street giants?'

To their eternal credit, her parents waited until the door was safely shut behind the housekeeper before they erupted.

'So this is the man,' her father stormed, waving the paper.

Soon afterwards Robert came in, and blustered, 'Wait until I get my hands on him.'

'You'll have the opportunity at exactly two o'clock this afternoon,' Judi retorted. 'He's calling for me then, to take me with him to Shropshire.'

Before she could start to explain the purpose of her visit there, her mother threw a calculated fit of hysterics, Robert slammed out of the house shouting, 'Good riddance,' and, typically, her father discovered an urgent business meeting which he had to attend.

Judi sighed. By now she was almost beyond caring what any of them thought about her. It was ironic that Nick shared their opinion. If they had only waited, they might have found themselves with an unexpected ally, she thought bitterly.

Only Lily appeared to see her point of view. The motherly woman, who used to be Judi's nurse, and from whom she had absorbed a very different set of values from those of her parents, slipped the newspaper into her hand when nobody was looking, and whispered encouragingly,

'You go your own way, Miss Judi. Don't worry. They'll come round quick enough when they find they can't use you for their own ends. A lot quicker than you would get over a wrong marriage. This one looks nice.'

Her approving look at Nick's photographed face made her championship plain, and nearly opened the floodgates again as Judi hurried upstairs and carefully cut out the picture to tuck into her handbag.

It was the only one she would ever have of them together. She was always alone on the pictures Nick had taken for the brochure. Which is what she would be, now, for the rest of her life, she mourned, and had to blot the blurred faces on the newspaper cutting, and shut it out of sight before it became irretrievably spoiled.

Promptly at two o'clock, Nick rang the doorbell.

Judi answered it herself. Her case was freshly packed and standing ready by the hall door, and as her feet propelled her along the carpet she promised herself, if Nick shouts at me as well, I'll scream.

Nick did not shout. His eyes went from her colourless, tear-stained cheeks to her ringless left hand, and Judi stiffened against the unspoken question in his look.

Her tight lips refused him an explanation of something that was nothing to do with him, and his face hardened in response to her silent resistance.

He asked her abruptly, 'Are you ready?'

Judi nodded, too choked to answer him, and he reached inside the door and picked up her case. She followed him dumbly to where his rakish, open-topped Jaguar, which she recognised as the one she had skidded into—was it only a few short months ago—made a scarlet exclamation mark on the drive that was more accustomed to her father's sober saloon.

'Get in,' Nick ordered her briefly, and for once Judi obeyed him willingly enough, and slipped into the passenger seat, while the capacious boot swallowed her luggage.

And then Nick was beside her, reaching round her to make sure the seat-belt was securely fastened; the accidental brush of his arm against hers brought back memory and pain, and a sense of desolation that wiped away all feeling, and left room only for the pain.

It hurt too much for her to appreciate the silent power of the big car, in which she would have delighted under any other circumstances. Nick had left the hood down, the windows were lowered, and the breeze flowing through her hair gave her a delicious sense of freedom as they left the Thames behind them, and turned north on to the motorway.

The car cruised effortlessly, and Judi turned up the collar of her coat against the crisp autumn air that was a cool contrast to the steamy heat of Bangkok. Out of the corner of her eye she saw Nick turn his head and glance across at her, noting her movement, and his hand reached out to the controls, and seconds later a cosy warmth flowed from the seat supporting her, radiating through her taut body, relaxing tensed muscles, and soothing away the trauma of the last twenty-four hours.

Nick's estimation of his own driving prowess had been no idle boast. His effortless control of the powerful machine reminded Judi of the mastery of a skilled horseman riding a thoroughbred. His light touch upon the wheel took them in and out of the traffic with consummate ease, while the luxurious upholstery cradled Judi in blissful comfort.

Nick touched another button, and soft music joined the sigh of the wind. Perhaps he preferred music to talking to her? Judi was beyond caring about his reason. Some of her favourite classics were included among the collection, and she closed her eyes the better to listen, and soak in the aural tranquilliser, using it to wash away the bitterness and recriminations of the last twenty-four hours, and clear her mind for the work which lay ahead when they reached Shropshire.

She had no doubt that Nick would be doubly demanding of her time and attention until the work was completed, and, however much she resented his dictatorial claim upon her services, it would have the advantage of distracting her thoughts until the job was finished.

Also, it would give her somewhere, temporarily, to live. After the row with her parents, Judi did not feel equal to returning home, to face the continued pressure which she knew they would exert without mercy to try to get her and Robert together again.

Even living in a hostel would be preferable to that. But in the meantime her stay in Shropshire would give her a breathing-space in which to decide upon her future, both with regard to permanent accommodation and a job.

It would be as pointless to go back to the language school as it would be to return to her parents' roof. She would be as easily accessible at the one as at the other, which made finding something to do as important as finding somewhere to live.

After her experience in Thailand, perhaps she might try travel agency work? she pondered. Dave would be able to advise her on her prospects in that direction. Her pride refused to allow her to ask Nick.

Thus dreaming, she drifted off to sleep, and awoke with a startled gasp when Nick shook her by the shoulder and said, 'It's time to eat and stretch our legs for a while, before we leave the motorway.'

'Where...?' Judi sat up, rubbing her eyes.

'We'll be home in another couple of hours, but you might not want food if you go without it for too long.'

'I don't feel like it now.'

'You will eat something, nevertheless. I don't intend presenting my aunt and uncle with a guest who's fainting from hunger. When did you last have a meal?'

His keen eyes raked her face, reading his own answer as Judi prevaricated, 'A while ago. I don't remember.'

She had eaten no dinner the night before, and her attempts at both breakfast and lunch were fruitless after Lily had produced the newspaper photograph. The last decent meal she had eaten, Judi realised with a shock, was their final dinner at the hotel in Bangkok, two whole days ago.

It restored her pride somewhat to believe that hunger might account for at least a part of the desolation which filled her, in which case she could remedy some of her ills if she could force herself to swallow a few mouthfuls of food.

She drew in a long breath and stepped out of the car, relishing the wide sweep of pastoral scenery that now took the place of the built-up areas on which she had closed her eyes. Refreshed by a quick wash and brush-up, she joined Nick in the restaurant a few minutes later, to find that he had already ordered their meal.

'Don't worry, it's English, not Thai,' he cut short her dawning protest, and the waitress nipped Judi's answer in the bud as she brought Nick's choice to the table.

Nothing could have been more English than the roast beef and Yorkshire pudding which sent messages to her deprived inner woman that, a short time ago, she would not have considered it was capable of responding to.

The first mouthful told her that she was ravenous, and after that she ate with a silent concentration matched only by Nick's wordless attention to his own meal on the other side of the table.

It struck Judi as strange that Nick should be so hungry as well. There had been nothing to spoil his appetite, unless he had been too busy since they had landed to spare time for more than a quick snack. Judi shrugged aside conjecture. Nick was a law unto himself. He would eat or not, just as he pleased, regardless of conventional meal-times.

Fortified by the food, she felt her strength returning, and with it her ability to fight back when Nick observed, over the coffee which followed, 'I see you're not wearing your engagement ring.'

Judi stiffened resentfully. What she wore or did not wear was nothing to do with Nick. She said tightly, 'It isn't mine to wear any longer. I gave it back to my fiancé. Ex-fiancé, now.'

'Did you give it back to him of your own free will, or did he insist upon you returning it?'

Judi reeled under his swift reposte. 'That was a rotten thing to say.'

'I notice your parents didn't come out to see you off. Have you told them you're coming with me, or have you taken off into the blue, the same as you did before?'

He was altogether too aware. Judi snapped, 'I started to tell them, and that's as far as I got.'

Nick scowled. 'Didn't you explain where you were going, and why?'

'Why the sudden concern for my welfare? They didn't show any. When I told them I was going with you to Shropshire, they didn't give me a chance to say any more. They simply refused to listen. They just jumped to all the wrong conclusions, and now they think the very worst of me.'

She could not resist adding, 'And probably you, as well,' and saw Nick's jaw tighten. But did not care as she rushed on hardily, 'So join in the Hate Judi Campaign. It seems to be spreading. If it makes you feel any better, my parents agree with all those things you're thinking about me, and all of you can't be wrong, can you?'

In spite of Judi's refuelled strength, her voice developed an odd crack in it, and, fearful that Nick would notice, she stiffened it resolutely, and crushed further questions with a pathetically dignified, 'I refuse to discuss my personal affairs with you. They are none of your business.'

If Nick started to question her, she feared that she might break down completely and make a fool of herself, but from a very different personal affair, which had nothing to do with Robert or her parents, and everything to do with her present companion.

Eating out alone with Nick again was doing disturbing things to her metabolism. Memories of those other meals together, when their love had turned the food and the wine into ambrosia and nectar, mingled confusedly with the tensions and undercurrents that ran like wounding darts across the table at this one, and one inescapable fact surfaced from the bewildering mixture to torment her.

Hating Nick did not prevent her from also loving him.

The discovery brought the threat of renewed tears alarmingly close to the surface, and to force them back she looked Nick straight in the face, and begged with a kind of brittle desperation, 'Let's talk about something more interesting.'

Nick fixed her for a long silent minute with a stare that seemed to stretch into eternity, before he shrugged and said, 'Suits me,' and piled pain on pain because he too was willing to condemn her unheard.

To counteract the agony, Judi pretended an interest she did not feel in the passing scenery, and by tacit consent they used it as a bridge to ease the strain between them when they resumed their journey.

As he drove, Nick talked, pointing out the various places of interest as the miles rolled behind them. He was as knowledgeable about his home country as he was about the Far East, Judi discovered, an accomplishment not always evident among the globe-trotting fraternity, and he captured her interest with the same ease as when they were in Thailand.

They left the motorway and turned west, and Nick explained another, much shorter spell of urbanisation with, 'We've just clipped the tip of Warwickshire. We're into Staffordshire now. Soon, we'll be over the border, and you'll see a marked difference in the countryside then.'

Shropshire announced itself with a road sign, and low green hills providing rich pasture for quietly grazing sheep, and sheltering deep valleys where already tractors were busily ploughing in the stubble from the recently gathered harvest.

Judi sighed, unconscious of Nick's eyes veering to search her face for the reason. The countryside beckoned to her, striking a hitherto unexpected chord deep inside her, adding to the agony of her longing for what could never be.

A gentle dusk began to soften the outlines of the woods and fields, blurring the one into the other with the onset of darkness, and distant, widely spaced pricks of light soon showed from isolated farms and cottages, reflected overhead in a dusting of early stars honed to a polished brightness by the crisp autumn air.

A larger glow of light ahead caught Judi's attention. It illuminated a low, timbered manor house, cradled on one side by the silver curve of a river; and she knew without being told that this was their destination.

Not a farm or a vicarage, as she had previously imagined.

Confirming her predictions, the car slowed, and passed between tall stone pillars, bearing armorial lions. Nick's birth sign. Judi threw him a startled look. Were they an ego trip on his part?

'Not guilty,' he denied gravely, latching on to her thoughts without difficulty. 'They've guarded the entrance to Compton Manor for a lot longer than I've been around. They're part of the family crest. You'll see them when we get inside. My uncle can't resist showing them off to all his visitors.'

'*His* visitors?' Judi echoed. She had not considered until now what her own accommodation was to be. She had vaguely assumed that Nick would put her up, considering the presence of his relatives under the same roof as being adequate chaperonage. Perhaps, holding such a low opinion of her, he did not consider a chaperon necessary to her good name?

'Yes. My aunt and uncle are looking forward to having you.'

Unable to help herself, Judi bit out, 'That's hard to believe, since I'm such a dubious character.'

'They only know that you're a member of the team, coming back to help me finish the job because of the tight printing deadline.'

'We'll meet the deadline, never fear,' Judi promised him grimly. 'I shall be as thankful as you to put the whole wretched episode behind me, and get on with living my own life.'

She had no idea of what that life would be, and the bleakness of not knowing frightened her, and it was made worse because Nick did not say, 'Don't be silly,' or any of the other reassuring things which other people might have said. Instead, he flashed back,

'Before that can happen, you've got a lot of work to get through. We both have. And it will only delay the job if you insist upon fighting me, so sheathe your sword, and let's concentrate on important things.'

Which showed all too clearly where she, Judi, stood in Nick's scheme of things. Work was all he cared about, she fumed. He was as bad as her parents, and Robert. His work came before anything or anybody. He was cold, hard and unfeeling; she hated him, and it showed in her brittle, 'That suits me,' as she threw his words back at him.

His steely glance told her that he recognised them, but there was no time for him to retaliate as the car stopped on the wide gravel sweep in front of the house, and an elderly couple emerged into the lamplight to meet them.

By contrast, their greeting was warm and friendly. Hugh Compton took Judi by the hand, and said, 'Welcome, my dear,' as if he really meant it, and Judi felt instantly drawn to this older version of Nick, and to his gentle, softly spoken wife.

She mourned the waste, since after her job here was done she was unlikely ever to see either of them again, and a few minutes later she followed Mary Compton upstairs to her room, with her mind a millrace of mixed feelings, as Nick dropped her suitcase on top of an old sea-chest at the bottom of the bed, and promptly disappeared.

Mary explained his going with, 'My husband is anxious for Nick to check on some renovation work we're having done to the stables. They'll join us afterwards for supper. It will give us time to get acquainted, and for you to make yourself at home.'

Her warm smile had done that already, and Judi's pleasure was genuine as she gazed at the low-beamed ceiling and panelled walls of the room that was to house her in the coming weeks, and the long window with its comfortable seat overlooking quiet parkland.

Unable to resist the impulse, Judi strolled across the room and looked out, excusing her action on the urge to see the view. She despised herself for the real reason, which was to catch a glimpse of Nick on his way to the stables.

Deliberately she turned her back when she caught sight of his tawny head rounding a corner of a building, faced the room again, and said politely to her hostess, 'I do hope I'm not putting you out too much, being dropped on you like this.'

'Not at all,' Mary returned promptly. 'We love visitors. We miss Nick when he goes abroad, although this time we've had a couple of guests staying with us for a day or two, which was pleasant. I'm glad Nick's back, though. There has been some sort of hitch about the work on the stable block, and Hugh likes him to make the decisions these days, since he will be taking over here eventually.'

'Nick's abroad a good deal, I believe?'

Judi tried to make her voice politely indifferent, but instead it came out asking a question, inviting further conversation on the same subject. Sternly she tried to tell herself that she did not want to talk about Nick, or to listen to things said about him, but the temptation was greater than her fragile strength, and she listened eagerly as Mary answered, 'He goes away much less these days than he did. He is taking on more of the running of the estate, as my husband finds it increasingly difficult to get about. Arthritis in an old war wound.' This explained the limp which necessitated Hugh Compton's resorting to the aid of a walking-stick.

Mary went on quietly, 'Nick loves the family home as much as we do, so we know it is in safe hands for the future. The manor is much too big these days for Hugh and me, and neither of us will be too sorry to move out to the dower house when the time comes.'

'Won't your husband miss his interest in the estate?'

'To some extent he'll retain it. His hobby is in regenerating the rarer breeds of sheep and horses, the ones that have nearly died out over the centuries, as newer breeds come along more suitable for modern needs. Hugh feels it is a pity to allow them to die out altogether. He's looking forward to concentrating all his attention on expanding his interest.'

'A happy ambition.' Judi smiled.

'It won't be too long before he's able to achieve it. We're planning to move out, just as soon as Nick gets married.'

CHAPTER EIGHT

As soon as Nick gets married . . .

How soon was soon? And who was the girl who was to be his bride?

The questions tracked backwards and forwards in Judi's mind through the long hours of the night, unanswered and unanswerable.

They drove her from her bed to pace the room, restlessly walking from window to door and back again, until at last, exhausted, she dropped on to the window-seat and rested her chin on her hands, brooding as she looked at the dark acres of parkland stretching, shadowy and mysterious, to the distant woods.

Through a gap in the trees she could just discern the outline of a square tower, a more solid darkness than the greenery; it must be the village church, where Nick would be married.

How soon? And who to?

Anger burned in Judi. Nick had accused her of being a butterfly, flitting from one man to the other, and all the time he was doing exactly that.

He was the moth to her butterfly, flitting from one girl to the other, vowing his love to her while at the same time secretly planning to marry another girl when he returned home.

What a perfect excuse it must have been for him, to use her engagement ring as a reason to quarrel and cast her aside, and blame it all on her. As always, he had been quick to take advantage of the situation to serve his own ends.

What reason would he have manufactured otherwise to make the break with her before they reached England? Judi wondered dully, and had still not found an answer long hours later, when the first pale streaks of dawn teased rags of mist from the river, and wrapped the trunks of the trees in a ghostly shawl.

Memories of that other, magical dawn they had watched together returned to torment Judi, and with a strangled sob she threw herself across the bed, seeking with shaking hands to blot it from her inner vision. She hurt too much for tears, and yet the memories must surely destroy her if she could not gain relief.

A tap on the door roused her. She pushed herself to a sitting position, and winced as her head throbbed a protest at the movement.

Daylight streamed through the windows, and she put up a weary hand to shield her eyes from the brightness, thankful that today, at least, they would betray no signs of her distress.

The weight of her unshed tears lay heavy on her heart, but there it could remain undetected by the outside world, and most important, by Nick, and she could salvage some of her pride.

The tap repeated itself, and a voice called, 'It's Violet, miss, with your tea-tray.'

Judi forced herself on to her feet and opened the door, and the fresh-faced country girl put the tray carefully on to the bedside table, and said, 'Mr and Mrs Compton don't get up until eight, but Mr Nick said you'd want to be early at work. Breakfast will be on the sideboard when you come downstairs, miss.'

Nick did not give an inch. Where had she thought that before? Judi wondered raggedly, and reached for the teapot as soon as she was alone again.

Her travelling clock said it was a mere five minutes past seven. What time did he expect her to start work? Eight o'clock? Office hours did not usually start until nine.

Which was the hour she would start, and not a second earlier, Judi decided rebelliously. Nick had forced her into coming with him to Shropshire to finish the work on the brochure, but she determined that he would not get things all his own way.

She felt ready to do battle again after her reviving cup of tea, and squared her slender shoulders as she marched downstairs half an hour later, ready for the confrontation.

A tempting array of salvers lay on the sideboard from which to help herself, but otherwise the breakfast-room was empty. She paused, deflated. After winding herself up to argue with Nick, he was not there for her to confront. She stood uncertainly in the middle of the room, and felt oddly abandoned.

Nick said in her ear, 'Good morning!'

Judi gave a gasp, and spun round. 'Don't creep up on me like that.' She heard her voice shrill, and hated the way his lips curved in amusement at the fright he had given her.

'What's the matter?' he gibed. 'Your conscience bothering you?'

'You...' She longed to hit him, but he was already out of her reach, calmly helping himself from the sideboard. As he conveyed his modest repast to the table, he threw over his shoulder, 'Aren't you having any breakfast?'

With an effort, Judi rallied her scattered nerves and remembered the mission on which she had been bound when she came downstairs. In a leisurely fashion she filled a cup from the aromatic liquid bubbling in the percolator, and when she about-faced again she had herself under reasonable control.

'There's plenty of time to eat between now and nine o'clock,' she answered him coolly.

She tensed against his reaction, which came with the speed of a whiplash. 'By nine o'clock you'll be too busy to have time to eat.'

Judi bridled. 'Office hours start at——'

'Office hours start when I'm ready, and finish when I feel like stopping. We've got a deadline to meet, remember. After the work is finished, you can get on with your own life, and work whatever hours you please.'

He did not add, 'Until then, you work the hours I choose, whether you like them or not.'

He did not have to. His steely look said it for him, and used her own earlier thrust as a stick with which to belabour her. Driven into a corner, Judi bit her lip.

To back down on her declared intention to leave Nick and his work behind her as soon as humanly possible was intolerable to her pride, and to give in to his demands was equally so.

Violet unwittingly offered her a face-saver. The maid came in laden with freshly made toast, thick and browned to a nicety. Glancing at it, Judi noticed that the bread bore long, thin marks of a paler colour, betraying that it had been toasted on the prongs of a fork in front of the kitchen fire.

She exclaimed, 'Skewered toast! I haven't eaten any done like that since I was in the nursery.'

Violet pursed her lips. 'These electric gadgets can't make real toast. I like mine crisp outside, and soft inside, with a bit of body to bite on, not thin as a biscuit, and all dried up. You might as well put butter on potato crisps as eat some of the stuff served up as toast these days.'

Her offering tasted as delicious as it looked. It was already generously buttered, and Judi accepted a slice and nibbled appreciatively, making it last crumb by crumb so as to stretch out the time until nine o'clock.

She still had a couple of inches of crust left in her fingers, and was wondering how much longer she would be able to make it last, when Nick said evenly, 'Every minute you spend eating after eight o'clock will tack a full hour on to the time you spend working this evening.'

Their glances met and locked across the table, determination crossing swords with defiance. Judi gritted, 'You can't make me work. I'll go on strike.'

'Newspaper reporters love strikes.'

Just as much as the reporter they met at the airport loved salacious titbits to print in his news-sheet. It was blackmail, no less.

'You're a monster,' she seethed impotently.

'I'm a man in a hurry. There's a lot to get through today. So let's get going, shall we? The earlier we start, the earlier we can finish.'

He drove her relentlessly throughout the morning. All the captions Judi had so laboriously typed in Thailand had been edited, and had to be retyped to fit in a strictly allocated space, with the wording suitably reduced where necessary.

Each alteration had to have Nick's prior approval before it was typed, and for speed's sake he came to work at the table beside Judi, and her heart contracted as his head bent beside hers over the page, and their hands touched as they grappled together to find the right words with the correct number of letters to fit.

No words were adequate to describe Judi's feelings as the electric contact made her drop her pen, and sent her mind blank, so that she fumbled with the typewriter keys, and had to erase and retype until in the end Nick snapped impatiently, 'At this rate, we shan't make any headway at all. Break for a coffee while I sort out the wording on this one, and then perhaps you'll be able to type at least one sentence without making a hash of it when you come back.'

The afternoon was even worse. The first lot of captions were completed, and they had to be matched up with the appropriate photographs.

Oh, the agony of sorting through the photographs with her own likeness laughing up at her from every one. The pain of the wish that would never come true, as a small bird flew free from its wicker cage, glorying in its release—but the magic had not worked for Judi.

Nick had printed an enlargement of each shot, and the detail on the superbly executed photographs made each memory of the scenes more vivid. Judi's heart twisted as he passed them one by one across the table to her, laconically describing them as, 'Shot number one . . . Shot number two . . .'

Had he no feelings at all? she wondered raggedly.

How could he view the small oblong pasteboards with such total indifference? Looking at them, she could smell the smells, feel the enervating heat again, and hear the happy, whispered words of love between them as they walked the sunlit streets together, stopping every now and then for Nick to capture her happy, smiling likeness against the exotic beauty of their surroundings, the miniatures of which trembled in her hands as she relived each moment of their brief togetherness.

She could hardly bear to look at them, remembering the ecstasy, and feeling the agony, and the pads of her fingers grew clammy with the effort, leaving her fingerprints on the corners of the photographs. Seeing them, Nick criticised her sharply.

'Have a care, or you'll spoil them. Hold them by the edges, like this. I don't want to have to do a second lot of prints.'

'There are two of a lot of them already.'

'The smaller set is for the travel brochure. We'll work on them first, to meet the deadline. The others are for my book. We can attend to those afterwards.'

'Your book?' Judi echoed. 'I didn't come here to help you with your book.'

It might take Nick all the winter to finish his book, and she could not survive seeing him every day for that length of time, loving him and hating him, torn in two between them, and knowing all the while that he was soon to be married. If she had to witness that event, Judi thought bleakly, she might not want to continue to live.

Desperately she objected, 'My contract was with the travel firm, to help produce their brochure, and nothing more.'

She would do just that, and only that, she vowed mutinously. Nick could not keep her a prisoner forever, using her as cheap labour. She would await her opportunity when he was not around and give Dave a ring, and get her future sorted out. When she shook the dust of Shropshire from her heels, she would need a landing-pad to aim at, which would give

her an added incentive to stand up to Nick if it came
to a confrontation when she left.

His look reached into her thoughts, and she shut
them off hastily lest he should read too much from
her expression as he retorted, 'Not so. I'm paying your
salary, so your contract is with me.'

If only it were. But Nick was talking about one kind
of contract, and she was thinking about another, and
the difference between the two suddenly blurred the
pictures in front of Judi, so that she was unable to
see clearly which one related to which caption, and,
guessing wildly, she mismatched two of them, and
earned another rebuke from Nick.

She snapped back, 'It's your own fault, for nig-
gling at me. I can't do anything right for you. If you'd
only go away and leave me to get on with the job in
peace, I'd manage a lot better without you.'

She would never be able to manage without him,
but somehow she would have to learn to come to terms
with the necessity, and the prospect brought back the
sense of desolation, made darker when Nick growled,
'You'll get your wish tomorrow morning. I'll be gone
before it's light, and I won't be back until after lunch.
So you might as well pack up for today and leave the
rest, if you feel you can do so much better without
having me around.'

His tone lashed her, and Judi wondered miserably
what was so important tomorrow to make Nick leave
his work, and risk breaking the printing deadline.

Should her question be not 'what', but 'who'?

Was he going to spend the morning with his future
bride? What else would he consider important enough
to drag him away from his work?

The question tormented her mind, and made it vir-
tually impossible for her to concentrate later that

evening, when Hugh and Mary took her to see the
sheep paddocks and the stables. Nick walked beside
Mary, while Hugh captured Judi, delighted to have a
listener who had not heard it all before.

He rode his hobby-horse with enthusiasm, but
Judi's distracted mind took in only half of what he
was saying, and when she had answered her host ab-
stractedly once or twice, and from Hugh's surprised
look gathered guiltily that she had probably said no
when it should have been yes, or vice versa, Hugh
pronounced, 'That nephew of mine is working you
too hard. You look tired out, you poor little thing.
Nick can be a positive slave-driver when he gets the
bit between his teeth. You really must learn to say no
to him when you've had enough, and mean it.'

What would Hugh say if he knew how much she
longed to say yes instead, and her whole lifetime would
not be enough to work beside Nick? Waves of agony
drove the colour from Judi's cheeks at the question
that Nick would never ask, and the answer that she
would never give. Hugh, noticing the effect, but mis-
taking the cause, ordered her gruffly, 'Have an early
night, my dear. We'll turn back now. I can show you
the rest another day, when you're less tired. Probably
tomorrow, after we all come back from Nick's lecture
in Shrewsbury during the afternoon. You'll enjoy that,
I'm sure.'

'I shan't be coming,' Judi objected. 'I've got to
finish the captions for the brochure.'

She did not want to go. Hugh's 'all' undoubtedly
included Nick's future bride as well, and her heart
contracted at the prospect of meeting the other girl.
It was quite bad enough loving Nick and knowing he
was to marry someone else, without having to meet
his bride face to face. It would be tantamount to

signing her own death warrant, and Judi's courage quailed at the thought of meeting her doom.

'As you will make such good headway without me being there to distract you in the morning, I'm sure you'll be able to spare an hour or two to come to the lecture.' Nick's sarcasm lashed her, and Judi's lips tightened against the angry rejoinder that pressed against them.

Once back in the house, she used Hugh's wrong diagnosis as an excuse to escape to bed, only to have her sleep disturbed by wild dreams of floating white bridal veiling, which she tried in vain to lift in order to discover what the face beneath it looked like, and she awoke early and unrefreshed to start her solitary morning stint.

Nick was already gone when she got downstairs, and there was no one this morning to criticise the time which she took to eat her toast; contrarily, she did not want any, which caused the ample Violet to scold her.

'You're slim enough, Miss Judi, without starving yourself. Half a cup of black coffee's no good to anyone as a breakfast.'

'I'll work up an appetite for lunch,' Judi promised with more hope than conviction, and escaped to the work-room in Nick's wing to apply herself to the unfinished work from yesterday.

The first set of pictures was gone from the table, and another batch awaited her in their place. Sorting alone through the vividly remembered scenes made Judi's eyes brim over, leaving a tell-tale smudge on a corner of one of the photographs.

She dabbed at it ineffectually, her pride cringing at the thought that Nick might see the smudge and guess its cause, and in a bid to cover up the mark she chose the largest paper-clip she could find, and attached the pasteboard to the appropriate caption in the hope that it would escape his notice when he returned.

Violet appeared with a tray of coffee and biscuits at eleven o'clock, and Judi wondered dully where Nick was having his coffee this morning. She imagined him leaning back in his chair, relaxed and smiling, chatting to his fiancée about his recent travels. Perhaps even planning to honeymoon in the very places where he had so recently declared his love for Judi.

The vision intruded between her eyes and the photographs, and in a desperate endeavour to put it to flight Judi reached for the telephone, dialled the number of the travel firm and asked for Dave.

Positive thinking, she rallied herself, but could not entirely erase the misery from her voice, when Dave's avuncular tones announced the older man on the other end of the line. Instead of the bright greeting she had planned, Judi found herself choking back the tears, and pouring out her troubles unreservedly into his receptive ears.

'Don't worry, Judi, love. I know of a vacancy coming up very soon,' he consoled her. 'There'll be a flat to go with it as well. You won't need it for a week or two yet, so that should fit in nicely. I'll be in touch nearer the time. Nick's only half-way through the brochure work yet.'

Judi put down the receiver before it occurred to her to wonder how Dave knew that, but she dismissed the idea of ringing back to find out. Nick was bound to be in touch with the travel firm, and considering the present state of her relationship with him he was unlikely to discuss details of his contacts there with her.

Feeling somewhat comforted by just hearing Dave's voice again, Judi returned to her work, re-checking what she had already done to ensure that there were no errors which might result in bringing down Nick's wrath upon her head when he returned.

The rest of the morning dragged interminably. Judi felt as if she had been working for a week when at last the solemn chimes of the hall clock released her to lunch with her host and hostess.

Nick had not returned. Probably he was lunching with his fiancée, and pangs of jealousy drove away the pangs of hunger, and earned Violet's further disapproval, so that Judi was glad to escape when the meal was over and go upstairs to her room to get ready for the trip to Shrewsbury.

Hugh drove them, and his sedate progress in the capacious family saloon was such a violent contrast to the exhilaration of a drive with Nick in his open-topped Jaguar that Judi emerged into the magpie charm of the ancient border town feeling as if she had just made her way there by means of transport almost as old.

Nick was already in the hall when they got there. He was chatting to two men who were helping him to set up cine equipment in a suitable spot aimed at a large screen erected on a raised stage at one end.

He looked up when Judi came in with Mary and Hugh, and her heart lurched, but he did not speak to her especially. His casual inclusion of her in his general, 'Hello, there,' hurt, as one of the electricians left what he was doing and escorted them to three seats in the front row.

Judi's eyes searched the line of chairs, seeking the girl who would one day be Nick's wife, but no face offered itself as a possible candidate. All the people already there appeared to be in pairs, and Judi took her seat beside Mary and Hugh, her curiosity unsatisfied.

She would find out soon enough, she decided drearily as the hall filled to capacity, and Nick was announced to his waiting audience as, 'Professor Compton, who has kindly agreed to give this lecture at very short notice, owing to Professor Broadbent's being unexpectedly detained.'

The lights went out, and Judi had cause to be grateful for the ensuing darkness to hide her expression as the film flickered, and then steadied, and a picture as clear as it was cruel settled on the screen.

Now she knew exactly what Nick's future bride looked like.

The girl's face was on almost every picture. Just as her own had been on the pictures Nick had taken in Thailand. She stared out at the camera, sweetly serene, her dark, wavy hair rippling almost down to her slender waist.

She was extraordinarily beautiful. And Judi knew, with a rock-like certainty, that this was the girl who was going to be Nick's bride.

Anger grew inside her as she fixed her eyes on the screen. How could Nick deceive a girl who looked like that? Compassion seized her as she watched the pictured face on each successive slide. How long would the sweet serenity remain, when she knew what Nick was really like, as inevitably she must find out one day, when he revealed himself in his true colours?

One day, that lovely face would be blotched by tears, as her own had been, she did not care to remember how often, and all because of the same man.

Judi never knew how she endured the next two hours. She scarcely heard a word of the lecture, only the sound of Nick's deep voice, ringing like a hollow knell inside her.

Only a word or two here and there caught her attention. 'Sung dynasty, AD 960 to AD 1279 . . .' and she realised that he was talking about China, and not Thailand. And then his voice stopped, and her ordeal was at an end as the audience rose to its feet and clapped uproariously.

In a daze, Judi followed suit, and clung closely to Mary and Hugh as they quit the hall shortly afterwards, ready for the drive back to Compton Manor.

She hoped they would start off right away. Nick would be busy in the hall for a while, dismantling the cine equipment and the screen and packing it all away in the boot of his Jaguar.

She did not want to speak to him. She loathed and despised him even more now after seeing the image of the girl who was being so cruelly deceived, and she did not even want to think about Nick until her anger had welded together the remnants of her poise, for they felt as shattered as the pieces of ancient porcelain pictured in one of his slides.

The crisp evening air restored her somewhat as they walked to the car park, and she agreed readily to Mary's suggestion of, 'Shall we give Heather and Llew a lift home? You won't mind squashing up a bit in the back, will you, Judi?'

Judi felt she would have sat on the car roof if necessary. Other people would mean general chatter about the events of the afternoon, and no one would notice if she was unusually silent.

Nick said from behind her, 'There's no need for anyone to squash up. Judi can ride with me.'

Judi spun round, unable to control the dismay on her face. 'You won't have room. Your equipment . . .'

'Broadbent has arranged to collect the equipment later. It's his, not mine,' Nick answered, and, taking her by the elbow, he propelled her towards the Jaguar.

The middle of a crowded car park was no place to start an argument, which bitter experience told Judi that Nick was bound to win anyway, and she fixed her eyes on the car as they approached it, studying its sleek lines in a failed bid to mitigate the wild emotions that made her blood run riot at the feel of his fingers clamped round her arm.

Nick intercepted her glance at the car, and misinterpreted it. He said drily, 'Your Mini didn't leave any scars.'

His car had remained unscathed, but the subsequent collision with its owner had left her, Judi, scarred for life, and the raw wounds throbbed as she got in reluctantly beside him. Nick keyed the engine into life, and turned out of the car park behind Hugh.

He was uncommunicative as they drove, seeming content to keep behind the older man's saloon, and copying his discreet pace, but the ride, which should have been one of peaceful enjoyment, became a dragging torture to Judi.

She, too, remained silent, her thoughts brooding on the dark-haired girl who seemed to ride like a ghostly passenger in the car with them, her unseen presence a tangible barrier between them.

At last they turned in through the gates of Compton Manor, to be greeted by Violet when they reached the house with, 'Mr Martin's come, and his wife. I've put them in the drawing-room.'

Mary exclaimed, 'How nice! They said they'd call back if they had time. They're the visitors who came to stay with us while Nick was abroad,' she explained to Judi, and turned to the photographer.

'You haven't met Martin's wife yet, Nick. If you remember, he got married while you were in Ceylon. Do come in and say hello.'

She hurried in front of them to the drawing-room, calling out as she pushed open the door, 'My dears, how lovely of you to come.'

Judi hung back, feeling distinctly *de trop*. The strain of the near silent ride with Nick was beginning to tell on her flagging reserves of self-control. If she had to endure his company for much longer, her anger would surely boil over, and she would tell him exactly what she thought of him, on behalf of the girl who was to be his bride.

With her mind in a turmoil, she did not feel capable of responding to small talk with strangers. Perhaps, after the introduction, no one would notice if she slipped away to the work-room. She had to brace herself to remain calm as Hugh drew her forward to be introduced to the visitors.

'Come and meet my nephew once removed. Martin, meet Judi. And this is Martin's wife . . .'

'*Louise!*' Judi gasped, and held out her arms blindly.

The one person in the world to whom she could unburden her troubles had appeared out of the blue, in the one place on earth where she was least able to take advantage of her friend's listening ear.

She blurted in a stifled voice, 'What are you doing here?' and Louise answered her, with a keen look,

'I could ask you the same thing.' She held Judi at arm's length and surveyed her face critically. 'You must tell me all about your holiday in Thailand.'

Her tongue spoke banal pleasantries, but her searching eyes wanted to know much more, and Judi ached to be able to tell her. What a relief it would be to unburden herself to someone who would listen to her point of view. She felt better already at the prospect. But first of all she must get Louise on her own. Her opportunity might come after dinner.

The meal dragged. Judi toyed with her food, and noticed dully that Nick seemed to have no appetite either, although he bore his share of the conversation, urbanely accepting his place as second host.

Was he grudging the time spent away from the girl with the dark hair? He had been ready enough to leave her behind to spend long weeks in Thailand, and to seek consolation to while away the time while he was there, Judi thought contemptuously.

Inevitably the talk centred on travel. Louise's husband was jubilant that the two had succeeded in reaching Scotland on foot during their holiday.

'We got as far as Dumfries before we had to turn back,' he rejoiced, and Louise put in ruefully,

'We were footsore by the time we got there. I've still got a blister on my one heel, but it was enormous fun. Martin wants to walk the length of the Pennine Way on our next holiday.'

'Aren't you glad you went to Thailand instead?' Nick enquired of Judi *sotto voce* as they repaired to the drawing-room afterwards for coffee, and Judi looked up, startled, to meet an unexpected twinkle in his eye.

He could actually remember the outcome of her trip to Thailand, and laugh about it. She longed to strike him but, denied the opportunity in civilised company, she had to content herself with a glare instead.

His callous amusement at her expense made up Judi's mind for her. When Louise left Compton Manor, she would go with her. Newspaper gossip could not be more cruel than being with Nick. She could avoid buying a newspaper, but there was no way she could hope to avoid Nick while she remained under the same roof with him.

She tried her best by deliberately sitting at the other side of the room when Violet brought in the coffee, but Nick selected a chair directly opposite to her, and his cool stare transfixed her like a butterfly on a pin.

Hugh suggested to Martin and Louise, 'Come and see my latest acquisitions. I've managed to buy a breeding pair of spotted sheep. Lovely creatures. Criminal to allow the breed to die out.'

Judi grabbed at the chance to go with them.

Here was her ideal opportunity to chat to Louise, while Hugh rode his hobby-horse, and engaged the attention of the men. She jumped to her feet eagerly, but Mary cautioned her husband, 'Don't walk Louise too far, Hugh. Remember her blistered heel.'

'She can come with me in the governess cart,' Nick offered promptly, and destroyed Judi's hope of buttonholing her friend for a private tête-à-tête.

She scowled her frustration, but perforce she had to walk with Mary, while Hugh expounded his hopes for the nucleus of his new flock to an attentive Martin.

After a while, the governess cart drew away from the party on foot, Nick explaining, 'I want to check on some fencing at the end of the park, while I'm out. You go on back when you're ready, and we'll follow you.'

They did not return for nearly an hour. Judi watched the clock anxiously. They've had time to build a brand new fence by now, she thought sourly, watching her opportunity to confide in Louise disappear as the minutes ticked inexorably by.

When the two finally returned, they were chatting and laughing as if they were already old friends, and Judi grew more and more disgruntled as Nick shamelessly monopolised Louise during the rest of the evening.

It was as if he sensed her urgency to talk to her friend, and went out of his way to foil her intentions, and Judi's nerves felt raw by the time Louise rose with a yawn, and said apologetically, 'You'll have to excuse me. I'm absolutely dropping.'

Was this her cue for a chat? Judi looked across at her friend expectantly, and felt baffled when Louise avoided her eye, and looked at her husband instead and urged, 'Come on, Martin. Don't keep Hugh talking half the night. Folks keep respectable hours in the country, not like us stay-awake Londoners.'

Judi's spirits sank to zero when Martin rose obediently, and amid general goodnights quit the room with his wife. Had she only imagined Louise's concern? She rose hastily herself as Mary and Hugh prepared to follow the example of their guests, and she had almost reached the door when Nick shot out a hand and detained her.

'We've got something to clear up before bedtime,' he said, and Judi swung on him angrily as the door shut behind her host and hostess, leaving her alone in the room with Nick.

'Whatever it is can wait until the morning,' she flashed. He had worked her until midnight once, and all for nothing, and she was determined not to be caught in the same way again. 'I've clipped all the photographs to the right captions. I double-checked to make sure, and I'm not starting on another batch tonight, whatever you say.'

It was easier to defy Nick, she discovered, now that she had made up her mind to go with Louise whatever the consequences.

'I'm not talking about work. There's something that needs to be cleared up between you and me.'

'Everything is crystal clear between you and me. You think I'm anybody's woman. You said so.'

'Judi, will you ever forgive me?' He reached out, caught her by the shoulders, and pulled her towards him, and Judi pulled back with all her strength, but it was not sufficient to combat his, and her eyes were wild as he moulded her to him.

She flung back into his face, 'I don't care what you think of me any more. When Louise goes home, I'm going with her, and you can tell that wretched newspaper reporter whatever you please. It doesn't matter a jot. So go ahead, and make up whatever stories you fancy. I'll survive.'

'I'm sorry. I didn't mean it.'

'I *do* mean it. And you'll be the one who's sorry in the long run. It won't be me who has to forgive you. It'll be the dark-haired girl on the slides you showed this afternoon. The girl you're going to marry. Presumably she reads the newspapers as well. Any stories you tell about me will include you as well. What will she think of those, I wonder?'

'The dark-haired girl on the slides? What has she got to do with it? I'm not marrying her.'

'Why not? Have you pushed her aside as well, for somebody else, as you pushed me?' Judi's voice cracked to a halt.

'I haven't pushed anyone aside. Caroline is Broadbent's wife. She had to go into hospital suddenly, because her baby started to arrive earlier than they expected. That's why Broadbent had to ask me

to step in and do the lecture for him. I don't date
married woman, any more than I date engaged ones.'

'I'd decided to end my engagement before I went
to Thailand. That's why Louise sent me, to think it
over...did you say, Professor Broadbent's *wife*?'

His words sank in, and Judi felt as if she had been
pole-axed. 'His *wife*?' she echoed, faintly. 'I don't
understand.'

'Neither do I,' he answered grimly. 'There are a lot
of things I don't understand. Or at least, I didn't,
until you rang Dave this morning.'

'How do you know I rang Dave?'

'I was in his office at the time. He told me why he
kissed you on the veranda at Chiang Mai.'

'He promised he wouldn't say anything to anybody.'

'There's a time to keep silent, and a time to speak,'
Nick paraphrased. 'Dave told me a lot of things, which
all added up.'

Judi blanched. 'What sort of things?'

'Enough to make me realise what a complete fool
I'd been. Except that Dave was a mite late. I'd come
to that conclusion already. Oh, Judi, Judi, my love,'
he groaned, and with a desperate strength that set
aside her resistance he crushed her to him, and covered
her face and hair with kisses. 'Forgive me,' he begged.
'I love you.'

'How can you say you love me, when you think all
those things about me?'

'I don't think all those things about you. I never
did. I only said them because I was hurt, and wanted
to hurt back. Say you forgive me. And when Dave
talked to me, and then Louise...'

'You listened to Dave and Louise, but you wouldn't
listen to me. Neither would my parents.'

'I went to see your parents before I saw Dave.'

'You *what*?' Judi stared at him incredulously. 'How did they receive you?' She wanted to know, and Nick slanted her a rueful look.

'With pointed pistols, at first. Then I explained to them who I was, and why you were with me, and by the time I'd had a talk with them, they were beginning to feel more than a little ashamed of the way they had treated you. Which made them more ready to listen when I told them I wanted to marry you, if you'd only have me?'

Nick's voice was a question, and his eyes were tormented with uncertainty as he waited for Judi to answer.

'You told them that, *before* you saw Dave? Before you knew...'

A warm glow started somewhere deep inside Judi, and began slowly to spread, melting her frantic resistance to his arms.

'I always wanted to marry you, right from the very first moment I set eyes on you. I haunted the car park for weeks after you skidded into me, in the hope that you'd appear again, but you never did, and I was so miserable because I couldn't find you that I grabbed at the chance of going to Thailand to try to forget you. It didn't work.' He grimaced. 'I was like a bear with a sore head with Pet and Dave. And then, when you walked into the hotel room that day, I thought I was having hallucinations.'

'And I thought I was on fire when I tried to eat the curry you ordered for me.'

'Not many girls would have had the courage to try it. I loved you more than ever for that.'

'Dave did warn me,' Judi conceded.

'I've got news for you. Dave and Pet are getting married, and setting up their own travel agency.

They're both weary of trekking round the world and living out of a suitcase. He told me to tell you. We're both invited to the wedding.'

'That must be the vacancy he told me about, and the flat.'

'Don't take either, Judi, *please*,' Nick begged. 'Marry me, and stay at Compton Manor, where you belong.'

Compton Manor... Mary's words came back like an icy douche. The warmth fled, and a glacial numbness took its place, and Judi's words stumbled through tight lips.

'You don't date engaged women, and I don't date engaged men.'

'I'm not engaged to anybody. I've already told you, the girl on the slides is Broadbent's wife. Ask Mary, if you don't believe me.'

'Mary told me that she and Hugh intend to leave the Manor, and live in the dower house when you get married. Why should she say that, if you haven't already got an understanding with somebody else, even if you're not actually engaged?'

'Oh, Judi, what a tangle we've got ourselves into.' Nick hugged her close, and incredibly there was laughter on his lips. 'When I left you at home the day we landed, I drove straight up here, and told Mary and Hugh I'd be bringing you to stay, and why.'

'To finish the work on the brochure.'

'I couldn't have cared less about the work. I told them that I'd blackmailed you into coming with me, because I loved you so much I couldn't bear to lose sight of you again. I was crazy with fear that you would go out of my life a second time, the same as you did before, and I couldn't bear it. And when Mary met you and talked to you, she told me she was convinced you loved me, too, even if you wouldn't admit it. That was all I had to keep my hope alive. That, and the picture of you releasing the bird at the Bangkok store.'

His voice was hoarse as he added, 'Did you wish that day, Judi, when you set the little bird free? What did you wish? Tell me.'

His lips sought the soft, trembling outline of her mouth, demanding an answer, but Judi hung back, still fearful of revealing her heart's most precious secrets.

'I don't remember wishing,' she prevaricated, and Nick shook his head, unconvinced.

'The photograph I took of you says you did. Photographs can't lie. Was your wish the same as mine, I wonder?'

Still she evaded him. 'The bird was too tiny to carry more than one wish.'

'If I'm right, he only carried one. The same wish, for both of us.' Gently he cupped her face in both his hands, a pale flower between his fingers that he tipped up to meet his eyes.

'Am I right, Judi? My wish was for you,' he told her simply. 'I loved you then, and wanted you for my wife. I love you now, and always will, right to the end of my days. There will never be anybody else for me, Judi. Will you marry me?' he begged her humbly.

His arms folded her close. His tawny eyes beseeched her, firing as he read the answer he wanted in the happy glow of her own.

'Tell me what you wished,' he urged, still needing to hear the answer from her lips, which he released reluctantly only long enough to hear her whispered reply.

'I wished the same as you. I love you, Nick. I didn't think the magic had worked for me. But now it has.'

With a happy sigh she lifted her lips to his, and only the soft sound of falling logs, crumbling into the ashes of the dying fire, broke the long silence as their lips fused, and passion spent itself as Judi answered kiss for kiss.

'Marry me soon?'

'As soon as you like.'

'Tomorrow?'

'Goose!' Judi laughed. It was incredibly easy to laugh, now. 'It can't be that quick.'

'I told you I was a man in a hurry. In a hurry to marry you.'

'Every bride has to make some arrangements.' Judi sighed again as she remembered the all-too-recent fuss at home, and Nick watched the cloud pass over her face, and with quick perception guessed its cause.

'Louise told me how you hated all the uproar at home before you left for Thailand.'

Judi said soberly, 'A wedding, to me, means the vows. The "until death us do part" bit. Not the outward show, like dresses, and bridesmaids, and a fashionable church.'

'That's what it means to me, too. So if you don't want bridesmaids, and a big reception, and all that jazz, let's elope.'

Judi shook her head. 'I want a white wedding. Every bride does. And I'd like Louise to be my matron of honour.'

'And the fashionable church?' Judi pulled a face, and Nick put in quickly, 'Let's get married here, in the village church. The one you can see through the trees from your bedroom. That way, each time we attend the services there, or look across the park to the tower, it will be like renewing our marriage vows all over again. Mary will do all the arranging for you. In fact, she's already offered.'

'Already offered? But she doesn't know...'

'Mary's a shrewd woman, for all her gentle ways. She was convinced all would come right in the end. I hung on to that conviction as if I were drowning, and it was the only lifebelt I had.'

'My parents will want a hand in it, too.' Judi's expression became anxious. 'I don't want to hurt them.'

'What a tender-hearted little thing you are.' Nick pressed ardent lips to her mouth. 'But don't worry. Mary will find a way to sort things out so that there aren't any bruises for anybody to nurse afterwards. She's a genius at keeping people happy.'

'In that case, the village church will be lovely.'

'So will you.' Nick smiled, the happy smile of a man who has just had his dearest wish granted. 'I've already got the silk for your wedding dress.'

Smiling down into Judi's startled eyes, he confessed, 'I bought yards of white silk from Jim Thompson's in Bangkok, the day you were choosing your own, in the hope that one day you'd wear it as my bride.'

'And now I will,' Judi murmured contentedly as she surrendered herself to his arms, happy in the knowledge that very soon she would repeat those words as she stood beside Nick in the village church.

HARLEQUIN
Romance®

Coming Next Month

#3073 BLUEBIRDS IN THE SPRING Jeanne Allan
After the death of her mother and stepfather, Tracy could have done without a bodyguard—especially Neil Charles. Attractive but arrogant, he clearly held Tracy's wealthy image in contempt. They sparred constantly but she fell in love with him just the same.

#3074 TRUST ME, MY LOVE Sally Heywood
Though it went against her nature, Tamsin had every incentive to deceive Jake Newman on her employer's behalf. Yet when it came to the crunch, she found that Jake's trust in her was the only thing that mattered.

#3075 PLACE FOR THE HEART Catherine Leigh
Florida real-estate developer Felicity Walden knows the Dubois family's Wyoming ranch would make a perfect vacation resort—but Beau Dubois refuses to sell. Still, she's convinced that a cowboy's stubbornness is no match for an Easterner's determination. Even though the cowboy is far too handsome for the Easterner's peace of mind....

#3076 RAINY DAY KISSES Debbie Macomber
Susannah Simmons knows what she wants—career success at any cost. Until she falls in love with Nate Townsend. But her five-year plan doesn't leave room for romance, especially with a man who seems to reject all the values Susannah prizes so highly.

#3077 PASSPORT TO HAPPINESS Jessica Steele
Jayme should have been devastated when she found her fiancé in another woman's arms. But there was no time to brood over the past. She was too busy coping with presently being stranded in Italy in the hands of attractive Nerone Mondadori....

#3078 JESTER'S GIRL Kate Walker
The moment he set foot in her restaurant, Daniel Tyson antagonized Jessica Terry. Though she reacted to him as a stranger, there were two things she didn't know. One was Daniel's unusual occupation; the other was that they'd met—and fought—once before.

Available in September wherever paperback books are sold, or through Harlequin Reader Service:

In the U.S.
901 Fuhrmann Blvd.
P.O. Box 1397
Buffalo, N.Y. 14240-1397

In Canada
P.O. Box 603
Fort Erie, Ontario
L2A 5X3

You'll flip . . . your pages won't!
Read paperbacks *hands-free* with

Book Mate·I

The perfect "mate" for all your romance paperbacks

**Traveling • Vacationing • At Work • In Bed • Studying
• Cooking • Eating**

Perfect size for all standard paperbacks, this wonderful invention makes reading a pure pleasure! Ingenious design holds paperback books OPEN and FLAT so even wind can't ruffle pages — leaves your hands free to do other things. Reinforced, wipe-clean vinyl-covered holder flexes to let you turn pages without undoing the strap...supports paperbacks so well, they have the strength of hardcovers!

Pages turn WITHOUT opening the strap.

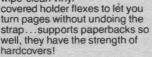

SEE-THROUGH STRAP

Reinforced back stays flat

Built in bookmark

BOOK MARK

BACK COVER HOLDING STRIP

10 x 7¼ opened.
Snaps closed for easy carrying, too